THE
ELEPHANT
MOUNTAINS

THE
ELEPHANT
MOUNTAINS

SCOTT ELY

ORCA BOOK PUBLISHERS

Library and Archives Canada Cataloguing in Publication

Ely, Scott
The elephant mountains / Scott Ely.

Issued also in electronic format.
ISBN 978-1-55469-406-8

I. Title.
PZ7.E574EL 2011   J813'.54   C2011-903486-7

First published in the United States, 2011
Library of Congress Control Number: 2011929252

Summary: A fifteen-year-old boy and a college girl struggle to survive after a series of
hurricanes has flooded the Mississippi delta and anarchy reigns.

*Orca Book Publishers is dedicated to preserving the environment and has printed this book
on paper certified by the Forest Stewardship Council®.*

Orca Book Publishers gratefully acknowledges the support for its publishing
programs provided by the following agencies: the Government of Canada through
the Canada Book Fund and the Canada Council for the Arts, and the Province of British
Columbia through the BC Arts Council and the Book Publishing Tax Credit.

Design by Teresa Bubela
Cover artwork by Juliana Kolesova

ORCA BOOK PUBLISHERS
PO Box 5626, Stn. B
Victoria, BC Canada
V8R 6S4

ORCA BOOK PUBLISHERS
PO Box 468
CUSTER, WA USA
98240-0468

www.orcabook.com
Printed and bound in Canada.

14 13 12 11 • 4 3 2 1

For Susan

ONE

Stephen lay on the cot on the screened porch and looked up at the stars. A mad din of frogs rose from the water only a few yards away, the house set up on pilings against its rise. He never thought frogs could make so much noise. It seemed to him that all the frogs in the world were in the marsh, whose network of channels, like the veins on the back of his father's hands, stretched away to the big creek that flowed into the Bogue Chitto that flowed into the Pearl that flowed into the Gulf of Mexico perhaps fifty or sixty miles away. The stars, whose names his father had been teaching him, were easy to see because there were no lights. There was a security light up on a pole, but they did not waste generator or solar power on that or on lights in the house.

Also they did not want to reveal their presence. He supposed there were lights in New Orleans on the other side of Lake Pontchartrain. That was where his mother lived. Or perhaps she was no longer there? Perhaps she had been evacuated? Perhaps the city was absolutely dark and people were going about the flooded streets in boats and, like him, looking up at the stars?

Stephen was not back in New Orleans because in June a big hurricane had come ashore there. Then a week later another one made landfall not far from the city and, like the first, tracked up into the Mississippi Valley. Simultaneously one was coming ashore in Georgia. Then there were the two, one right after the other, in South Carolina. All made their way inland to areas drained by the Mississippi River. The one in Georgia went all the way to Ohio. The rain fell for weeks from these slow-moving, powerful storms.

The river rose higher and higher, and finally the river control structure failed. It was a dam and spillway system that once kept the Mississippi from entering the Atchafalaya River above New Orleans and creating a new path to the Gulf. Now most of the river flowed through what was once the Atchafalaya. Because of the rains upstream, there was still plenty of river flow past New Orleans and Baton Rouge.

From New Orleans to the high ground near Natchez, everything was underwater. The population had been evacuated. As more water came down the Mississippi from the rains inland, it became less and less likely anyone was going to return soon. The National Guard and the regular army were stretched very thin. Their attention was required for the two wars in Africa and a much larger one in Asia.

Some people stayed. Since the National Guard and the local police had abandoned the little towns, the result was that those stay-behinds did whatever they wished. His father called that anarchy, stealing some gasoline or fresh water from someone and perhaps killing him if you were in the mood. His father liked to say things like that happened routinely in other places in the world, and now Americans were finding out the true nature of human beings. Stephen did not know if that was true. He did not want to believe it.

Stephen kept getting conflicting and wild reports from the various radio stations. One in New Orleans claimed the new levees the Corps of Engineers completed, the ones to replace the levees built years ago in response to the big Hurricane Katrina, were holding and were in absolutely no danger of being overtopped or breaking. Other stations said the levees on the lower Mississippi had been overtopped in many places. Creeks and small rivers that under the levee system did not run directly into the Mississippi now did. As one report put it: "Things have been rearranged." One station out of

Texas claimed that the whole coastal plain from Texas to South Carolina, including New Orleans, was underwater and was going to stay that way for a long time. Florida had simply vanished beneath the sea, the victim of a series of big hurricanes and sea levels that rose faster than anyone thought possible. The same was true throughout the world. It was also hot, the climate going from temperate to tropical in just a few years.

The station he liked the best was one he could not place geographically. There were no commercials and no call letters, just a voice. The man spoke with a deep Mississippi accent and called himself the Swamp Hog.

"*Listen, children, listen,*" the Swamp Hog said. "*Move inland. This ole hog can live in a swamp but not you. Move to the Himalayas. Move to the Andes. Move to the Rockies. Good Lord, but it's turned hot. Soon those mountains will be covered with the thickest jungle you've ever seen. The sea is rising. Get yourself where it can't reach you.*"

He wanted his father to listen to it, but he was never able to bring the station in when his father was present.

"I think you're dreaming that station," his father said.

"No, it's real," he insisted.

"It's the station of anxiety. Everyone has one of those broadcasting twenty-four hours a day. Up in their heads."

He would carefully adjust the dial but was rewarded for his efforts only with static.

They were able to live comfortably. The generator and solar panels kept the freezer going, filled with meat, mostly venison, wild hog and fish. One room in the house was completely filled with steel drums containing rice and beans. When he lived with his mother in New Orleans in the house near Audubon Park, she occasionally referred to his father as "that crazy survivalist." But he never thought she really meant those words. She was an impulsive woman, laughing one moment and crying the next. Sometimes he would study the girls at his school to see if any of them showed signs of growing up to be like his mother. It would be good to be able to tell early and avoid them.

His mother and father divorced when he was a baby. Now he was fifteen. His mother had done well as an investment banker in New York. When he turned ten, she retired to New Orleans, where her family had lived for a long time. There were some relatives still about, mostly old people who used canes. The ladies' kisses left damp spots on his cheeks from their rubbery lips. They smelled of powder and perfume. The old men offered wrinkled, clawlike hands for him to shake. It was through them that his mother became deeply involved in Mardi Gras. Then she took up designing costumes. A young man of twenty-five or so, who he suspected she did not sleep with in the four-poster bed in the second-floor bedroom, came over regularly throughout the year to look at her sketches.

"Courtland is a genius with a sewing machine," she liked to say.

Even then he could tell she was not satisfied with her retirement, with Mardi Gras, with him, with any part of her life.

He was never sure who he might meet when he came down for breakfast, prepared by Josephine, the young Cajun woman his mother hired to cook and clean. Josephine liked to sing and had a good voice. He enjoyed hearing her sing as she cooked, standing there chopping peppers, her clear pure soprano filling the house. She drove him to and from his school. He liked his school and wondered if it was underwater. He played defensive back on the football team. So he would come downstairs and one of his mother's young men, who painted or played music, might be having breakfast by himself or sometimes with his mother. Sometimes with Josephine. He might see that particular young man for a few weeks at breakfast, but he would come downstairs one morning and the man who played the saxophone would be replaced by a man who painted or wrote poetry.

He knew what they did in her bedroom at night even though he had not done that yet. To the members of the football team he tried to give the impression he was knowledgeable about girls. No one ever challenged him even though he did not even have a girlfriend. He was more interested in football and baseball than he was in girls. Josephine said that soon he would be interested in girls. His mother said the same thing. He thought Josephine knew more about him than his mother. It was Josephine who came to his football games and who took him to the doctor when he was sick. The older boys made jokes about her and hinted she was more to him than a nanny. He hated that word. Those boys were careful to use it as much as possible.

Then his mother began to talk of sending him to military school. That was fine with him, just as long as they had a football team. He decided he might like wearing a uniform and marching around. After all, his father was once a soldier. His father fought in the Iraq War, before he was born. He did wonder why she wanted him gone. Josephine said that military schools were for bad boys, but he had never been in any sort of trouble. Although she was opposed to his going, she did not have a vote.

"Am I a bad boy?" he asked Josephine.

"Why, hell no, honey," she said. "There's no bad in you. You just keep going to your nice school. Then to college."

By college she meant Louisiana State University. His mother had other choices in mind.

He could not recall seeing his father at any time when they lived in New York, but he did come to New Orleans to visit once or twice a year and took Stephen fishing at the mouth of the Mississippi. He always wondered if his father was perhaps more interested in catching red fish or sea trout than in seeing him. His father drank beer and got a little drunk and joked with the boat's crew. Those men seemed to like his father, and he suspected it was not just because they were getting paid. He watched carefully, thinking he could learn to imitate his father's easy way with those men.

Then his mother stopped talking about military school and made the decision for him to spend the summer with his father. She did not bother to ask him how he might feel about that. The day he found out, they were all having breakfast at the Café du Monde. He had returned from the bathroom, where his mother had sent him to wash the powdered sugar off his hands, and found them in the middle of a conversation.

"We agreed at the beginning you'd have Stephen in the summer," his mother was saying.

His father shrugged.

"You were happy with the way things were, Anna. Why change them now?"

He wondered why he had never spent a summer with his father when that was the agreement.

"He'll love spending the summer with you," she said.

She put her arm around Stephen and gave him a hug. Involuntarily he felt himself stiffen. He imagined those young men putting their hands on her and felt a wave of anger sweep over him. This had happened before, but usually he could control himself better. And there were some of those young men he genuinely liked.

"You all right?" she asked.

"Yes, ma'am," he said.

She removed her arm and took a drink of her coffee.

"I've got work to do," his father said.

"Well, you can teach him about motors," she said.

He knew his father did repairs on outboard motors. Maybe he sold them too. It was not something they talked about on their fishing trips.

"Don't blame me if he ends up being a mechanic," he said.

"Oh, I'm not," she said. "Only *you* would throw away a good education." She turned to Stephen. "Did you know that your father has an engineering degree from Georgia Tech?"

He shook his head.

"Good Lord, Anna," his father said. "Did you carry around a list in your head of the best schools in the country when you were fifteen years old?" He took a drink of his coffee and smiled at her. "Well, maybe you *did*."

Stephen lay on his back on the cot and considered what he had learned. It was September now and instead of being back in school with his friends or marching around at some military school, he was here with his father. He had learned about outboard motors and airboat motors and guns. Along with the drums of rice and beans, there were cases of assault rifle ammunition. He had learned to shoot rifles and pistols and shotguns. He had learned to hunt and fish. It seemed to him there was no better way to live than the way they had been living.

There was no sign, as far as he could tell, of a woman ever being in the house. He could imagine how a woman like his mother might transform it. He could picture Courtland sitting at a sewing machine, yards of material trailing about on the floor, as he sewed furiously. If his father had a woman friend, he kept that a secret. Stephen did not think that would trouble him. He just preferred having his father all to himself after all those wasted years.

At first he thought his father was exaggerating when he called it a "paradise." But he had come to agree with him. Before the hurricanes started coming, they would get up early in the morning and have coffee on the screened porch and watch the sun rise over the feathery-topped cypresses lining the big creek. Then the light would fall on the marsh, all those little channels shining in the light, and he thought that was the prettiest sight he had ever seen.

He wanted to remain with his father. His parents had discussed that. His father had met his mother in New Orleans to talk about it. He had been able to tell things had not gone well. His father was sad.

"What did she say?" he asked.

"You're stuck with her until you're eighteen," his father said.

"She doesn't even want me there."

"If a person gets the idea you're taking something away from them, they get real interested in that thing."

He did not like his father using the word *thing* to stand for him, but he knew that his father was just giving him an example.

"Does she still want me to go to military school?" he asked.

"She wants you in New Orleans," his father said.

His father looked old and tired. He was staring down at the floor, obviously thinking about something. Stephen waited for him to speak.

"You go back to New Orleans and have a good year at school," his father said. "Study hard. You can spend the whole summer again next year."

He was pleased that his father wanted him back.

"And interceptions," his father said. "You'll have more this year."

"Yes, sir," he said.

For some reason, after this summer, he thought that he might look on his mother's young men differently when he met them at breakfast. He would think of them putting their hands on his mother, but that would not be the same either. He resolved that this year he would have a girlfriend. He would know exactly what his mother and those men did in the bedroom. And that knowledge would further change how he regarded them, move him closer to being an equal.

But then all those expectations and disappointments were wiped away when the hurricanes started to arrive. His mother and father talked on the phone about his staying through the first one. Then his mother seemed to prefer that he remain with his father when the second one approached.

"She hired that security service," his father said. "Nothing like a few former Navy Seals hanging around to make you love a hurricane."

The security people were there to protect the valuable furnishings of the house.

"Nobody's going to carry off a single piece of furniture, not a single painting," his father said.

But then the phone service failed, and his father had no more conversations with her.

He was delighted he was stuck. He wished the march of the hurricanes across the Gulf would never stop.

Even work was not really work. They did not go into town to his father's shop anymore because the town and the road that led to it were underwater. They had been working on the engine of his father's airboat, moored at the dock in the marsh. Its 454 Chevy big block engine had been running rough. His father thought it was the carburetor, and they rebuilt it, but the engine still ran rough and sometimes would not start at all. So they were going to have to go into town in the johnboat and hope they could find a carburetor that had not been ruined by the water at his shop or the auto parts store. They could walk right in and take one off the shelf at the auto parts store since the town was evacuated two weeks ago. The thought of going into the deserted town and taking the carburetor instead of paying for it filled him with excitement.

He supposed his father, a wonderful shot, had learned to shoot during the Iraq War. But he found it hard to get his father to talk about the war. He did persuade him to reveal that he was in a "special unit." But nothing much beyond that. He liked to imagine his father parachuting into the desert wearing night-vision goggles. His black parachute was like a piece of the night sky. Silently floating down amid enemy soldiers who had no chance at all.

He wondered how many men his father had killed. But that was a question he knew better than to ask.

"But what was it like?" he asked.

"Sand," he said.

"Sand?"

"Yeah, lots of sand."

He heard his father begin to snore from where he slept on the couch just inside the door to the porch. His father was partial to sleeping on couches, dropping off to sleep with a book in his hand. His mother had complained about that habit. He wondered if he had bad dreams of the war, dreams of sand. But he had never heard him cry out in his sleep or wake suddenly from a nightmare. His father slept with a MAT-60 submachine gun. Stephen liked it that now he knew the names of weapons like that. He imagined himself sitting on a bench in the locker room at his school and casually mentioning the rate of fire of that French machine gun. His father wrapped his arms around it as if it were a woman. He wondered if his father slept with the machine gun when he and his mother were together. He could not imagine any of his mother's young men sleeping with a machine gun. But perhaps they did now, that is, if New Orleans was filled with anarchy.

To Stephen anarchy was nothing more than a word until last week when they discovered a man's body in the big creek with a bullet hole in his head. The man was dressed in a business suit. It was the first time he had seen a dead person. As they sat there in the john-boat, Stephen wondered how they were going to get him aboard without turning the boat over. He thought perhaps the best plan was to let him stay right where he was. But he did not say any of this to his father. Stephen knew that dead folks were supposed to be buried.

"Shouldn't we bury him?" he had asked.

"No, we don't have time to bury everything that's dead around here," his father said.

Stephen supposed his father had seen plenty of dead people, and now they did not bother him at all. The dead man did not bother Stephen that much. He had not been in the water long enough for the turtles to get at him. He looked like if they towed him to shore and stood him on his feet he might wring out his clothes and walk away and nobody would know he had been dead at all.

His father gave the body a push out into the current with a paddle blade. It paused, spun slowly and then floated off down the creek toward the river only a few miles away. Stephen wondered if it would float all the way to the Gulf. He imagined the man's bones coming to rest in deep water, lying there in that absolute darkness forever. It was then he realized they were not living in paradise after all.

"I learned about killing people in Iraq," his father began. "You have to be careful."

He stopped and looked off down the creek. The body had disappeared. Stephen thought he was going to tell him that it was kill or be killed if a soldier planned on staying alive. His father then continued in a voice so low Stephen had to listen carefully.

"You cut yourself off from those you kill," his father said. "They're just targets. But if you push too hard on that, then you cut yourself off from everyone."

"Everyone?" Stephen asked.

"Yes, from love. Do you understand?"

"Yes, sir."

But he did not understand. His father's comment about war being equated with sand made just about as much sense.

"We don't know what we'll have to do out here," his father said. "Be careful."

"Yes, sir," Stephen said.

Stephen wanted to ask his father a thousand questions but decided to keep silent. It seemed to him that his father was expecting trouble, and the thought of that both attracted and repelled him. His father had been tested in Iraq. Now it was his turn.

Stephen reached down and felt the barrel of the Saiga-12 under his cot. The Russian-made combat shotgun had a twenty-round ammunition drum and a skeletal collapsible stock. He had fired it many times on his father's shooting range.

"Just keep shooting, even when they're down," his father cautioned him. "Even with double-ought buck it won't be as easy as you think."

He wondered what it was going to be like if they had to defend themselves. They were only five miles from the little town where his father had his boat shop. Everyone knew they had ample stores of food and fuel and water, all commodities worth killing for. His father liked to say that they now were living in a world in which anything was permitted.

They were all right during the storms because his father had built the house to withstand them. His father liked to say that if a tornado hit the house it would just bounce off and go on its way. The pilings the house sat on were steel, not wood. The house was made of concrete blocks over a steel frame. It was attached to the pilings with special tie-downs, and the metal roof was secured in the same way. Steel hurricane shutters protected the windows and the screened porch. So even the hurricane that hit them directly did no damage, although it made more noise than he thought was possible. And when it was over, they had fresh water from the big storage tank fed by a cistern. His father had released a few snapping turtles into the cistern. He liked to say you can't have a cistern unless you have a turtle or two in it.

The water was filtered when it came out of the cistern, so the turtles would not do any harm. They had plenty of gas and diesel fuel in big underground storage tanks.

As he closed his eyes and drifted off to sleep, he found himself imagining holding the shotgun in his hands and firing at the dead man in the creek, who now was alive and bringing up an assault rifle on him. The shotgun recoiled against his shoulder, the ejected shells spinning out, their brass bottoms gleaming in the sunlight. The man's rifle barrel was swinging upward, but then the force of the buckshot caught him and he tumbled backward, like a wide receiver Stephen had laid a good hit on. His coaches had praised him for his willingness to hit much larger boys.

"Good boy," he heard his father saying in his dream as he drifted off to a dreamless sleep. "Good boy."

TWO

L ate one afternoon Stephen put on waders and followed a deer trail to the edge of the marsh to try to shoot a couple of ducks. They would have them the next day for dinner. He took up a stand hidden from the house by a tree line and well concealed from approaching ducks by the marsh grass. He tried to stay still. He watched an alligator swim across the marsh to the creek. A banded water snake swam by a few feet away. Dragonflies darted about among the marsh grass. At dusk he expected to ambush some wood ducks when they came in to roost, or perhaps a teal.

He willed himself to be motionless, like a cypress stump or a clump of marsh grass, to be separate from time, to step out of the flow. It was something his father had taught him to do.

"Don't even think about time passing," his father told him. "Ignore it. Then you can wait. Most people can't do that."

He could not imagine his mother waiting for anything. She was not good at that. Then he felt bad for thinking things like that about her. She had worked hard in that bank; she had taken care of him.

He pushed the thoughts of his mother into some distant recess in his mind. He watched the play of the sunlight on the water, a ripple that could be a gar or an alligator or a snake. He imagined being a dragonfly sitting on a stalk of marsh grass, looking at the world through its faceted eyes.

But by the time the sun slipped behind the trees and it began to grow dark, he had still seen no sign of a duck.

He heard a motor in the creek. Pretty soon a powerful light was shining among the cypresses and then out into the marsh. Someone had come up from the river. He'd had been told over and over if someone showed up he should hide himself and let his father deal with intruders. By now Stephen expected his father had heard them too and seen their light, so he would be ready. He carefully walked out of the cover of the trees and into the marsh a little way so he could see the house.

The boat slowed to a crawl. The searchlight played over the house, but there was no sign of his father. Then they reached the dock, and someone cut the engine.

"Walter," someone yelled. "Walter."

The light disappeared. He took that as a bad sign. The men in the boat had decided not to expose themselves. Were they friends of his father? They knew his name. He could not see anything, just the outline of the roof of the house against the lighter darkness of the night sky. The moon was not up yet. His father did not reply.

"Walter," a different voice called, this one not as deep.

He heard the whistle of wood ducks overhead, along with the thrum of their wings. Then there were splashes in the marsh. The ducks had gone to roost at the last possible moment. Almost at the same instant, the shooting began, most of it from AK-47s, but then there was also the sound of his father's machine gun. Someone began to scream, the sound so terrible he clapped his hands over his ears. He just hoped it was not his father. He thought again of his father's instructions: if something like this happened he was to stay away. His father would come find him. If he did not come, that would mean he was dead.

But it could be his father screaming. He started along the trail that wound through underbrush and high grass. Because it was under a foot of water, he had to move carefully so as not to make noise. The screaming faded away to a few murmurs and then stopped. Now he was out of the water, and it was easier to be quiet. Then the searchlight came on again. Through the trees he could see the figures of three men. None of them looked like his father. Three bodies lay on the ground.

He sat down and slipped out of the waders. It was going to be impossible to move silently in them. Ahead of him was a clear sandy area. They would not be able to see him approach because they would be blinded by the light. He wished he had the Saiga-12 instead of the Browning filled with duck loads. He took out two shells and held them between the fingers of his left hand so he could reload quickly. The shotgun held one in the chamber and four in the magazine. The men were talking, but he could only catch a word here and there: "ammo," "gas," "Walter." One of them kicked at a body with his foot. They all laughed.

Now he was moving forward at a crouch. He was just about to enter the edge of the circle of light, the men no more than twenty-five yards away. He eased off the safety of the Browning. As he took a deep, slow breath to calm himself, he thought of his dream-fight with the dead man in the creek. And he found himself lost in that dream so that the two things, the dream and the men standing in the clearing, bled into each other. He stood motionless, watching it happen as if they were being projected on a giant screen before him. His legs and arms felt heavy. He could not imagine he would have the strength to bring up the shotgun. As he took another deep breath, he heard the sound of his own heart beating. He pulled himself away from the sound and its hypnotic effect. The men and the night around him sprang into sudden sharp focus as if his body had been awakened and propelled into action by a sudden electric shock.

He ran toward them, his bare feet making little squeaks in the sand. The man closest to him turned toward him, and—just like in his dream—he saw him raise his rifle. He put two shots into the man's chest. The man crumpled. The other one was firing, and he heard the bullets zip by his head. Suddenly the light went out. Had a stray round hit it? Was there another man in the boat? He shot the man before him too and tried desperately to bring up the shotgun on the third man. The removal of the light had reduced the man to a dark figure standing before him. Stephen realized that the third man had had plenty of time to kill him. But when he turned toward him, he saw the man was fumbling with his rifle. It was jammed.

Stephen swung the barrel of the shotgun up to the man's chest. The man dropped his rifle and held his crossed arms over his face.

"Don't!" he screamed. "Please! I didn't shoot him! I can't! It's jammed!"

For the first time Stephen realized his father was lying facedown in the sand only a few feet away. Now that Stephen's eyes were beginning to adjust to the darkness, he could see the dark outline of the submachine gun by his side.

"I didn't!" the man continued to say. "I didn't!"

Stephen turned back to him and brought up the shotgun.

"No!" the man cried. "No!"

It seemed it should be easy to pull the trigger, to empty the shotgun into him. Vengeance for the death of his father. But he found he could not.

"Walter was my friend," the man said.

Stephen almost shot him for that.

"I want to see your face," he said.

"What for?" the man asked.

Stephen did not have an answer for that. He had already pulled the mini-flashlight out of his pocket. He pressed the button and shined the light on the man's face. He was a little redheaded man wearing an Atlanta Braves cap. His skin was a pale white. Stephen imagined he must be one of those people who never tanned. He had had his nose broken at some point in his life. He was breathing hard as if he had just finished a race. Stephen felt as if he had been looking at him for a long time, but he knew that it could not have been more than a few seconds. He turned off the flashlight.

"Get out of here," Stephen said.

The man was gone in an instant. Stephen heard his feet on the sand and then on the dock. The motor started, and the johnboat moved out along the channel toward the creek.

Stephen now regretted he had not shot him.

He would've killed me if his rifle hadn't jammed, he thought.

Then he turned to his father. It seemed that none of this could be real, that any moment his father was going to come out of the house, angry at him for disobeying his instructions. Stephen resisted the temptation to lose himself in that dream, and again sand, the insects, the hot sticky air, the scent of his own sweat overwhelmed the dream. He reached out and put his hand on his father's back. He was still warm. But he knew this kind of stillness, the face in the sand, could only mean death.

He rolled him over, not an easy job. Stephen felt wet spots on his chest and back where the bullets entered and exited the body. In the daytime he would be looking at his father's blood, bright against his khaki work clothes. He was glad the face was unmarked, or at least he thought it was. He reached into his pocket for the flashlight but realized he had dropped it. He would go to the house for a gas lantern. He ran his hand over his father's face and felt no wounds, only sand. He brushed it away. Then he touched his father's face again, feeling the stubble of his beard, the strong thrust of his arched nose, his square chin.

If he had not gone hunting, this might not have happened. He imagined coming to meet the men with his father. The two of them might have survived.

No, I'd be dead too, he thought. *There were too many of them. Or I could have started shooting when they came into the marsh. But they were out of range. Too far. Too far.*

Crying took him by surprise. It came as a relief. He listened to his sobs as a counterpoint to the choruses of frogs. He lay on his back beside his dead father and wept as the moon rose over the cypresses along the creek. Some of his killers were dead, but he found no satisfaction in that. He realized he was going to have to bury them along with his father. If he did not, they would rot and stink. Vultures would fill the yard and roost on the roof of the house.

He got up and blew his nose and wiped his eyes. Then went to the house for a lantern and a shovel.

After he lit the lantern, he placed it next to his father's face. He was right. It was unmarked. A cloud of insects, mostly moths, danced around the light. He sat there for a long time looking at his father and brushing away the moths that settled on his face. Then one by one he looked at the faces of his killers. They were unshaven, rough-looking men dressed in the same sort of work clothes his father wore. One had his name, Ed, stitched on his shirt. He wondered if they ever did anything criminal before the hurricanes arrived. They looked like ordinary working men. But like his father they had stayed behind deliberately, in their case to loot and kill.

He began to dig his father's grave. It was not difficult going in the sandy soil but still hard work. It took him a long time, and he did not like to have to think about his father lying a few feet away while he was doing it. The lantern was running low on fuel and beginning to flicker, its circle of light gradually diminishing. He realized he should have filled it before he started. He hated to just roll him into the grave, but he had no way of lowering him gently. When he pushed the body into it, it landed with a heavy thud.

"I'm sorry, Father, I'm sorry," he said.

His voice sounded unusually small and insignificant. When he turned off the lantern and looked up at the sweep of the stars overhead, he felt even smaller. And he was not really sure what he was sorry about except that he was duck hunting when his father was murdered. He stood by the side of the grave and cried for some time before he worked up the nerve to drop the first shovelful on him.

When he swung the shovel out over the grave, he paused, the blade with its load of sand suspended over his father. He delayed the moment of dropping it, a moment when his father seemed not dead and the grave did not yawn before him. But it was going to be impossible to hold everything in suspension. He could not stay frozen over the grave, not even for five more seconds. So he gave the shovel a little twist in his hands, and the sand dropped, the weight on his arms gone, and the load fell onto his father's body with a heavy *plop*.

After the first, the next one was much easier. He wondered if he should say some words over him now or wait until the grave was filled. He decided to keep working. So he applied himself to his task and shoveled with a methodical regularity, dropping shovelful after shovelful into that rectangular patch of darkness.

When he dropped the last shovelful of sand on top of the little mound that had risen over the grave, he tossed the shovel aside and took off his sweat-stained work gloves. He sat down on the sand, breathing hard. For the first time in his life, he wished he had been in the habit of going to church, because there he might have learned some words to say.

"Now you won't ever have to leave paradise," he said.

That sounded foolish, especially set against the croaking of the frogs and the insistent mindless hum of the insects. But somewhere, deep in the swamp, whip-poorwills were calling, and he knew his father would like that. And maybe the calls of those night birds were better than any words he or anyone else could say.

He calculated it would take him the rest of the night to bury the others. He considered pouring gasoline on them, but he knew it would take an extraordinary amount of gas to consume the bodies. He did not have it to waste. He sat down and cried again, out of despair for what lay before him. But then he thought he had a solution. He would use the johnboat to tow them to the creek. Once in the current they would float down to the river to join the dead man in the suit, turtles and catfish their undertakers. He recalled his father's words about there being too many dead things to bury.

So he dragged them to the water. He roped them together, heads to ankles, and then brought the john-boat from the dock and tied the free end of the rope to a cleat. He started the engine and carefully towed them into the nearest channel. He was surprised that his plan was working so well. He considered how, at the beginning of the summer, this scene would not have been a part of his wildest nightmare.

I killed them, he thought. *How can that be?*

And he discovered revenge was sweet. In fact, he wished he could kill them over and over again. Now he understood why sometimes men at war mutilated the bodies of their enemies.

Once at the creek he worked the boat through the line of cypresses and towed the bodies out into the slow but powerful current. He steered the boat upstream so the bodies were strung out behind him. The motor strained as it felt the tug of them. He put the engine in neutral, took out his knife and cut the rope. He played a flashlight over the bodies as they floated off down the creek, thankful they escaped becoming entangled with the timber on the flooded banks or the midstream snags.

○ ○ ◡

Back at the house he stood over his father's grave. This time he did not cry. He did not think he had a tear left in him. Again he tried to think of the right words to say, but nothing came. He knew there was a burial service in one of those church books, but despite all the books in his father's bookcases, he had never seen one like that.

By the time he lay down on his cot, it was well after midnight. He picked up the Saiga and lay it beside him. He tried to close his eyes and sleep but found even closing his eyes difficult. He should not have spared that man. All the things they killed his father for were still right here, and at any time that man might collect a new group of looters and come back to take them.

Now there was just his mother. She at least was safe, protected by the security people who had been paid to take care of her along with the paintings and furniture. He considered how she would react when she learned of his father's death. He supposed he would be the one to tell her. Would she cry? Would she laugh?

He wondered what it would be like to just stay here, live alone. After all, his father had lived out here alone for a long time, first in a tent and then in a trailer. He had built the house himself.

No women. He realized that could not be true. His father was a man like other men. He was building a myth of him for reasons he did not understand.

No, I have to go back, he thought. *She's my mother. She might need help.*

And he realized he could now give her real help. He knew how to shoot. He had killed. He would be like an extra security man. He recalled his father's words about the dangers of killing, the words he did not completely understand. He did not think they would apply to him. He lay there turning these things over his mind, examining them from various angles. Giving up on sleep, he lay there wide awake, waiting for morning, when he would walk out to stand by his father's grave.

But even though he thought he would never go to sleep, he finally did. He woke to the birds' morning songs, the shotgun cradled in his arms.

THREE

He had breakfast on the screened porch and considered his options. But his mind kept returning to thoughts of his father. He imagined how good it would be to see his father, returning from a morning hunt in the marsh, come walking along the edge of the water, his shotgun in one hand and a duck in the other. It was pleasant to indulge in such a dream, but he suspected doing things like that would make it all that harder to accept that his father had died brutally not forty yards away. He did hope his father had not been the one who was screaming. The location of the wounds in his chest suggested he had died quickly.

He turned and looked at the grave. He realized he had sat with his back to it. He wondered if he had done that on purpose. The grave was unmarked. He had considered what might make a good marker, but he could not come up with anything. All that came into his mind were things like engine blocks or tools. They would mean something to him, but people would laugh when they saw the grave decorations. Yet his father deserved some sort of remembrance. He would think about that.

He thought again of the man he let escape returning. He suspected his mother would have been in favor of him killing all of them. She would have done it herself if she had been there and known how to shoot. That man he spared and his friends could come in the night when he was sleeping, and he would not have a chance. Maybe if he had a dog? But the only dogs he had seen were dead ones.

After he ate he went out and looked at the grave. The first rain would wash away the patches of blood on the sand, and future rains would level the mound. He turned and looked toward the creek, wondering if the bodies he dumped there had already made their way to the river.

He would repair the airboat and go to New Orleans and find his mother. Those security people she had hired would keep her safe, but he could imagine them abandoning her if things got too bad. His father would have wanted him to go. He wondered what the difference would be between the security people and his mother's collection of artists. Former Navy Seals would be—unlike most of the artists—athletic men, the sort of men who were the stars on their high school football team.

By now she had probably installed one of them in her bedroom. And that seemed to him something that should not disturb him. His mother was doing nothing wrong, breaking no promises or vows.

So why does it bother me so much? he thought.

He was less disturbed with the thought of her in bed with one of the security men than with one of the artists.

He recalled his mother taking him in bed with her when they lived in New York. He must have been about four or five. He had been sick and kept waking with fever and nightmares. That recollection of her scent, that woman-smell of perfume and scented soap and flesh, different from the scent of men. Then there was the heat of the fever and the soft feel against his body of the cotton sheets. They were a cluster of sensations that every time he was in her presence seemed to hover about her. In her absence he could call them up anytime he wished.

If she was not there, perhaps someone in the neighborhood would know where she had gone. Surely by now troops were in New Orleans and there was order. Getting the carburetor should be easy. He did not expect to find anyone in the town.

So he loaded the johnboat with extra fuel and water and food for a few days. He took the Saiga and plenty of ammo and an AK-47. He poled the boat out of the marsh and then along the flooded road that was marked by power poles. As the road neared the bridge over a tributary of the big creek, he started the motor and eased the boat along the flooded road. Soon he reached the paved road that ran into town. It had several feet of water over it, and he was able to run the boat at a slow, steady pace, watching out for debris.

He came upon a body in military camouflage and steered around it and then another and another. Bloated carcasses of cows and goats were scattered among them.

So this was what it was like, he thought. *My father must have viewed scenes like this in Iraq, although not watery ones.*

He realized there was no difference between the dead men and the dead animals. They were just dead. He recalled his father's words about the danger of cultivating an indifference to the dead.

Vultures sat on the power poles. In the middle of a flooded field was a dead tree filled with them. He did not expect they could feed on dead things in the water, but they would have a feast when the water went down. It made no difference to them whether they were eating a goat or sitting on a dead man's chest and dining on his liver.

His father's shop, unfortunately built on low ground, was a little outside of town. Someone had stolen the boats from the fenced lot beside the shop. He saw where they cut the fence. That was not surprising. Boats had become a precious commodity. The water was still up to above the top of the door. He did not even bother going inside. But the auto parts store was on high ground, and he was hopeful. He expected some water. It all depended on which shelf they kept the carburetors. He hoped it was a high one.

As he approached the auto shop, the water got shallower. He became even more hopeful about a successful trip. As he turned a corner, he saw a red canoe, paddled by a girl, moving up the street away from him. She was working hard with the paddle as if her life depended on putting some distance between them. He opened the throttle a little and caught up with her easily.

He used the boat to block her passage, forcing her into a chain-link fence. She tried to back the canoe out and escape.

"Whoa," he said as he put the engine in neutral. "Just wait."

She put down the paddle and turned to face him. She was dressed in a pair of chest-high waders whose top came almost up to her neck. Her face was covered with sweat from the exertion of paddling on the hot day.

She bent over and picked something up from the bottom of the canoe. When she turned back to him, she held a butcher knife in her hand.

"Don't worry," he said. "I won't hurt you."

But she was still scared, so scared she was trembling and breathing hard, taking in great gulps of air. She looked at him closely and then gradually grew calmer.

"Why, you're just a boy," she said.

"I'll be sixteen in December," he said.

"Do you have any water?"

He tossed her a full canteen. Her hands shook as she unscrewed the top. Then she started gulping down the contents.

"Careful," he said. "Don't drink too fast."

But she ignored him. He guessed she was twenty, maybe a little older. It was hard to tell with her dressed in waders and one of those broad-brimmed hats decorated with flowers women used when they gardened. She finished the canteen and sat there breathing hard.

"More," she said and tossed him the empty canteen.

"In a minute," he said. "You'll make yourself sick."

"I've had nothing to drink for two days."

To let her know that he had plenty of water and more was coming her way, he started to fill the canteen from one of the big water coolers. He took his time doing it.

"I'll give you this," he said. "But you've got to promise me that you'll just take sips."

She nodded her head and reached out for the canteen. He tossed it to her. To his surprise she did as he asked.

He asked what she was doing in the canoe.

"Looking for some bottled water," she said. She pointed at the muddy water. "If you drink that, you'll die."

They both looked at the trash-strewn water around them. Here and there were oil slicks.

She told him her father owned an appliance store in the town.

"When everybody left, he decided to stay. To protect his washing machines. The store is in an old building downtown and has a second floor and an elevator. He moved everything up there. We all thought the water would go down in a few days."

She went on to tell him that their house was close by, on high ground, and they thought they could live upstairs. They were running low on food and water and getting nervous because the water was rising, not falling, when one day she heard the sound of a motor.

"I thought it was the National Guard," she said.

She had been in the attic and was preparing to come downstairs to investigate the motor when she heard a shot and then her mother's screams. Then there were two more shots. She heard the sound of men laughing.

"I knew they'd be coming up to the attic," she said.

But there was a place to hide, a secret room her father had built for her when she was a child, concealed behind a fake wall.

"Just like in the movies," she said. "You push this hidden button and the wall swings away."

She had sat there in the dark on the floor of the tiny room, no bigger than a closet, her arms wrapped around one of the stuffed animals from her childhood.

"They rummaged around the attic for a while," she said.

One wanted to set the house on fire, but the others talked him out of it. That would just call attention to themselves. Any military helicopters in the area might come to investigate.

"I heard them leave," she said. "But I sat there on the floor for a long time. I cried but tried to do it silently just in case one of them stayed behind. Finally I decided they weren't coming back. I had to go downstairs."

She described finding her parents' bodies. Her mother had fallen in an awkward position across a chair. One hand was thrust upward as if she were trying to turn on the lamp. That was why the men had laughed.

He told her about his father and how he too had cried.

"I think maybe there're no more tears left in me," he said.

"Me too," she said.

She had no way to bury her parents so she abandoned the house and went to live downtown in the store.

He told her about the purpose of his trip to town and that he was planning to use the airboat to go to New Orleans. He explained to her that his mother was there, the house protected by security men.

"You come with me," he said.

"I'd be crazy not to," she said. "Your family must be rich."

"She's got paintings and furniture to protect."

"Like I said your family is rich."

He supposed what she said was true. His mother had done well in New York. She had told him she had done well. But his father had not had money. He built the house himself. He worked long hours repairing outboard motors and boat engines. It seemed to him his father was much happier than his mother.

She climbed into the johnboat and took off the waders. She was a plain-looking girl. He could smell the unwashed stink of her. Her brown hair was greasy and matted. He might not even recognize her if she had a shower and put on makeup and a dress. He still could not tell exactly how old she was, only that she was considerably older than he.

"I'm Angela Marks," she said.

Then he introduced himself. She recognized his father's last name.

He put the motor in gear, and they went off down the flooded street to the auto parts store. When it came in view, he was pleased because there was only a foot or two of water in the doorway. He put on his waders. He took the Saiga in case somebody showed up. His supply of water would be a good enough reason to kill them.

Inside there were some parts cartons floating about, along with the swollen body of a dead man. He smelled pretty bad. Stephen made his way around him carefully, not wanting him to start breaking up and smell even worse. He went behind the counter and back into rows of shelves where the parts were stored. He had to go down four rows before he found the carburetors. They were on a shelf just within his reach. He also took a couple of water pumps and some belts, because these were things that could easily break and would be impossible to repair. Then he retraced steps past the stinking dead man, whose bloated body bobbed a little in the slight wake his passing made. Now he saw the wisdom in his decision to tow the bodies to the creek.

The trip back was uneventful. The dead soldiers and cows and goats were still in the same place. The vultures were still patiently watching. Angela looked at the dead men as they passed, the boat's wake causing the bodies to bob. At least here in the open there was not much of a smell. He hoped Angela was not thinking of her parents.

Then Angela turned from the dead men to look back at him.

"The dead stink," she said.

"I know," he said.

"My parents are like them."

He had no idea what to say so he just nodded. He wanted to say that they were dead, that now it did not matter. But he thought better of it.

"Don't you think so?" she said.

He hated it that she was pressing him. He wondered why she would ask him a question like that.

"They're dead," he said.

"Yes, they are," she said.

He opened the throttle a little.

"You watch out for trash," he shouted. "I don't want to run into somebody's dead cow."

She turned around and fixed her eyes on the water ahead of them.

By the time they reached the house it was late afternoon. He brought the boat up to the dock slowly, looking for any sign of the return of the man. He did not want to tell Angela about him. His letting the man escape would make him look foolish.

Perhaps he had enough time before dark to install the carburetor.

"If you wish, you can take a shower," he said to her.

"You have a shower?" she said.

"And plenty of water and power to heat it."

He told her he would switch on the water heater and then go work on the engine.

○ ○ ◡

It was almost dark when he finished with the engine. When he turned it on, it purred, no sign of any problem. He walked up the steps and smelled something cooking. She had found the leftover venison stew his father had made. She had transformed herself into a nice-looking girl, not exactly pretty but nice-looking: brown hair that was close to blond, nice breasts, long well-shaped legs. She looked good even dressed in a pair of his shorts and one of his T-shirts.

"Those clothes of mine need to be burned," she said.

They ate dinner on the screened porch. As they ate the stew, he could not help but think of his father. When he made the stew, he had complained that he had no carrots. He never had any luck growing carrots in his garden.

She told him she was a senior at LSU, majoring in math. Her parents had expected her to become an accountant, but she wanted to have an academic career.

"They weren't pleased with that," she said. "There's no money in it. My daddy pointed that out right away. To him those washing machines were the most important thing in his life. Now he's dead because of them. And nobody tried to steal a single one. Those thieves were after other things."

He recalled that his father had never seemed particularly concerned about the fate of the shop.

"My father cared about this house, not those boats and motors," he said.

"Smarter than my father," she said.

She sighed.

"I guess I'm being too hard on my father," she said. "My mother didn't want to stay. She told me. But I'll bet she didn't say a word to him."

"He did the best he could," he said.

"I suppose."

She looked toward the airboat moored at the dock.

"Your mother'll be surprised when you drive up," she said.

He did wonder how his mother would react but did not speak of this to her. He was going to have to tell her his father was dead. She might laugh. She might cry. But she would not react in the way a normal person might.

"She'll be surprised all right," he said.

"She won't be glad to see you?" she said.

He told her about his mother's plans to send him off to military school, how she and her father never got along. And then he explained about all those young men.

"Better than old ones," she said.

She laughed, and then he did too. Her indifference to the spectacle his mother was making of herself with those young men made him consider that his reaction was not a reasonable one. And he looked out into the darkness and wondered if there was someone out there listening to their laughter. He had not turned on any lights, and she had not asked any questions about why he had not.

"You worry about those men of hers a lot?" she asked.

"I guess," he said.

"It sure sounds like you do."

"What if it were your mother?"

She began to laugh.

"My mother hadn't had sex with my father in years," she said. "Who was going to be interested in her? She sure wouldn't be interested in them. I'll bet your mother is beautiful."

Talking about sex was making him uncomfortable. He decided to work hard to make sure he gave no sign it did.

"I guess," he said.

"Don't you know if she's beautiful?" she asked.

And he wondered if somehow she knew that he knew absolutely nothing about sex and women. She could be playing with him.

"She's beautiful," he said.

"I expect she is," she said. "Maybe she wants to send you to military school because she likes you too much."

"What do you mean by that?"

"Oh, I don't know. You're a nice-looking boy, her only child. She might feel that it's time to let go of you."

He was thinking of his fever breaking and feeling cold and how his mother wrapped her arms around him and stroked his hair.

"What are you thinking?" she asked.

"Nothing," he said.

"I wonder," she said.

"Sometimes people don't think anything at all."

"Oh, is that so."

"Yeah, sometimes it happens to me."

Then she began to talk about herself. She told him how she planned to go to graduate school in mathematics. He wondered exactly what it was you studied after studying math for four years.

After a while she stopped talking. There were tree frogs on the screen, giving their calls over and over, their voices tiny compared to the deep voices of the marsh bullfrogs. Big moths bumped against the screen from time to time. She began to yawn.

He pointed out they would need to stand four-hour watches. He also explained why it was not a good idea to show any lights.

"No use getting killed on our last night here," he said.

"Ironic," she said.

"Do you know how to shoot?"

She told him she had never shot a gun. He decided this night was not a good time for her to learn.

"I'll take the first watch," he said.

She went off to sleep in his father's bed. He sat on the porch with the Saiga beside him and listened to the frogs and the night birds. After a time he got tired of sitting and went out to his father's grave. He stood over it, trying to think of something to say, but could find no words.

He found it was true he had no more tears, at least not at this moment. He wondered if he would be able to come to this place in ten or twenty years or if the sea would rise and put everything around him permanently underwater. It would not be so bad for his father to have a grave at the bottom of a warm shallow sea.

When he went back to the house, he decided to stand a double watch and let Angela get some sleep. She was exhausted. Besides, standing watch would give him time to think about the best way to get to New Orleans. The most direct way would be across Lake Pontchartrain. But then they would be vulnerable to the presence of speedier and more powerful boats, boats constructed to deal with rough water. The airboat was designed to run in a few inches of water or even a heavy dew, as his father liked to say. And the airboat would be overloaded with gas and water. He planned to find a route where the water was shallow and those other boats could not go. His plan was to follow the highway to the lake and then work around to the west end of either Pontchartrain or Lake Maurepas. He was not sure how long it might take to make the journey. It would be slow going through the swamps. But at least the danger of being ambushed would be greatly diminished.

He sat on the screened porch, thinking about these things, as the hours of his double watch wore on.

FOUR

He woke to bird songs. Angela was pulling her watch, sitting in a chair and looking out on the marsh.

"Do you always sleep with that gun?" she asked.

He explained how he started doing that after they killed his father.

"It makes me feel safe," he said.

He did not tell her about his father sleeping with the machine gun. She would not understand. He had never really understood, but now that he had killed the men and his father was dead, he did. It seemed like a normal rational act.

"After Mother and Daddy were killed, I slept with that butcher knife," she said.

So perhaps she did understand.

"I saw that picture of you with your parents," she said. "Your mother's beautiful."

Josephine had taken the picture of them standing together on the front porch of his house. Early in the summer his father had enlarged it and tacked a print to the wall over his bed. Stephen had wondered why he did that when there were no other pictures of his mother in the house. Over the years other pictures had been taken, but he had not chosen to display any of those.

After breakfast they loaded the airboat. He took plenty of ammunition and all the weapons, along with water, food and fuel. He took a little gas camping stove and some cooking utensils. When he tried out the GPS, he found it wouldn't work. He wondered if it was a problem with the machine or if the service had been blocked or lost. Somewhere in the house was a compass, but he couldn't find it. He took the radio. The report on the hurricane this morning from the Texas station was that it was going to make landfall somewhere in Mexico. He tried the mystery station but only pulled in static. He had never had much luck with that station during daytime hours.

Before they left, he stood with Angela at his father's grave. Her parents were unburied, still in the house, their corpses rapidly decomposing in the heat. He hoped she was not thinking about them.

"We should put up a cross," Angela said.

"He wouldn't like that," he said.

"You mean he didn't believe in God?"

"No, he didn't."

"I'll pray for him."

She looked down at the grave. He wondered how many people she had seen buried. For him, his father was the first one. She turned to him.

"And you. What do you believe?"

"Same as my father."

"I'll pray for you too."

It seemed to him she was going to be wasting her time praying over people who didn't believe. He didn't imagine the men he killed believed in much of anything. But he kept all this to himself. He didn't know exactly what a person was supposed to do when someone said they were going to pray for you and you had made it clear to the person doing the praying that you didn't believe in that person's god or any other god.

"Thank you," he said.

She looked like she was getting ready to say something but changed her mind. She just stood there, looking down at the grave.

Then she spoke.

"Do you think your mother will ever come visit his grave?"

"Probably not," he said.

He wondered if she was thinking of her parents, lying there rotting in the house. It would be a kindness, he thought, if the vultures came in through, say, a broken window and devoured them. She would return and there would be nothing but clean bones left. Or if the house washed away or burned. That would be good too.

"And you?" she asked.

He told her of his vision of his father's grave covered by a warm shallow sea.

"I like that," he said.

"Me too," she said. "There could be coral. And those fish with all the colors. The water would be very clear."

"Yes, I can see that."

He imagined schools of bright-colored fish hovering over his father's grave. That was a pleasant daydream. But it made him vaguely uncomfortable that she was participating in his vision.

"Sharks too and huge rays," he said.

"To stand guard on his grave," she said.

Then he realized they were both becoming too fanciful. And unexpectedly this did not feel like a good cure for grief.

He went to the shed where they kept tools and welding equipment. It was set up on steel pilings just like the house. He used a cutting torch to cut a rectangular piece, about the size of a license plate, out of a sheet of steel. Then he formed his father's name, *WALTER COLE*, from pieces of wire and welded the letters to the steel. He welded the plate to a steel pipe and took it out to the grave where he drove it deep in the ground with a sledgehammer.

"No hurricane will bother this," he said.

"We should say something," she said.

He went to the house and got his father's copy of *The Iliad*, his favorite book. They stood together at the foot of the grave while he read a passage from the account of the funeral of Patroklos. "'And let us lay his bones in a golden jar...,'" he began. After he finished he felt satisfied. He thought his father would be pleased. But Angela was not pleased or satisfied. She stood there and said some sort of prayer under her breath. He could see her lips moving. He kept his mouth shut and tried to be respectful.

They boarded the airboat, and he started the engine. It ran beautifully. They went out to the flooded road and headed for town. They would be able to pick up the highway to Lake Pontchartrain there. The bodies and the vultures were all exactly in the same place. When they went down Main Street, Angela pointed out her father's appliance store. He hoped she did not want to visit her house.

In the center of town he turned the boat onto the highway that led toward the lake. He placed Angela in the bow to look out for debris and ran as fast as he dared.

They went through one flooded little town after another and did not see a single person. Before long, the water was over the tops of some of the houses, and they floated cautiously over the submerged towns. In the countryside they came upon dead animals and an occasional human corpse. He was beginning to think this was going to be easy. He had feared what they might meet up with in one of those little towns. Besides the problem of running into people who might want to kill them, there was the additional worry that they would encounter stranded people in need of food and water. They had only enough for themselves. But it would be hard to say no to desperate people.

Late in the afternoon, when he calculated that they were close to the lake, he ran the boat up into a cypress swamp and went several hundred yards into it until they were concealed from the highway. They had yet to see anything of Interstate 12. There was a good chance it was completely underwater. Parts of it might have been washed away. They ate some sandwiches he had made for supper.

As he rigged up the mosquito netting he had brought along, he cautioned Angela not to show any lights. They would be able to hear the sound of a motor before anyone got close to them. No one was likely to come into the swamp at night.

Once it was dark Angela went to sleep under the netting. He sat in the padded driver's seat, the Saiga within easy reach. He picked up the radio and cranked the generator. Then he set the volume very low and dialed in the mystery station. And it came in, perfectly clear. He was tempted to wake up Angela but decided against it. The Swamp Hog told him the levees were breaking everywhere along the lower Mississippi. And New Orleans was finally flooded. But Baton Rouge was still mostly all right.

"*New Orleans is now the city in the sea,*" the voice said.

Then the Swamp Hog started reading a poem:

"*Lo! Death has reared himself a throne*
In a strange city lying alone
Far down..."

But his voice began to break up, and Stephen could hardly understand a word he was saying.

"*Apocalyptic Poe,*" the voice announced.

After that there was nothing but static.

The hours passed, and he woke her for her watch.

"Wake me if you hear or see anything," he said. "Just people moving about. I don't need to know about alligators or turtles or snakes."

She said she understood.

It seemed that he had just closed his eyes when he felt her shaking him.

"There're lights," she said.

He got up and saw the lights off toward the highway. They were far away and looked as if they were moving away from them. He heard the sound of a motor. Then he heard shots, from an automatic weapon he could not identify. The lights went out, and the sound of the motor faded and disappeared.

"Can you hear it?" he asked her.

"No," she said.

They sat there for a long time, not talking, listening for a return of those threatening sounds. But the only thing they heard was a splash somewhere from deep in the swamp. It was probably a turtle sliding off a log, or an alligator. He went back to sleep; she returned to her watch.

In the morning they had rice and beans for breakfast. That was safe because the camping stove did not put out any smoke.

"I wonder if people down here are going to live like this for a long time," she said.

"What do you mean?" he said.

"I mean if the land stays flooded and the sea comes up."

"You mean doing whatever they wish?"

"Yes."

"It won't be many people."

He told her it seemed to him that new boundaries between land and water would be established. The army would restore order. He wondered what sort of people would return to what was essentially a new country. There would be opportunities.

"I guess those washing machines belong to me now," she said.

"You'd run the store?" he asked.

"No, I expect I'll sell them. Bury my parents. Go someplace where it's dry."

He wanted to tell her that by the time she returned there would not be much left to bury. But he saw nothing to be gained by pointing that out.

Instead they sat quietly talking for some time about the new country that would take shape after the water receded. He considered telling her of the Swamp Hog's prediction of jungle-covered mountains but changed his mind. She was going to have to hear the voice first. If she did not, she would think he had gone mad.

He decided to teach Angela to drive the airboat so he could take a position in the bow with the Saiga. Unfortunately she would be exposed, sitting up high in the driver's seat, but he could not shoot and drive at the same time. Depending on her to drive was going to be a safer bet than depending on her to shoot.

Following his instructions, she eased the boat through the cypresses toward the highway. Once they reached the highway, he could see nothing but trees and water and sky. He let her continue to drive so she would have more practice as they headed toward the lake. He sat in the bow with the Saiga beside him and watched the water before them for debris.

They had not gone far before he saw up ahead something moving in the lower limbs of a big live oak. It was probably a raccoon or a possum. But then, as they came closer, he saw it was a human figure. He picked up the Saiga and pointed toward the tree. Angela nodded her head to let him know she had seen it too.

The figure, he could now tell for sure it was a man, stood up on the thick limb and waved both arms above his head. Stephen motioned to Angela to ease them in slowly and then told her to make a circle of the tree. She did that well. He got a good look at the man, who appeared more frightened than dangerous. After they made two circles of the tree, it was clear nobody was setting an ambush for them. The tree was not filled with riflemen. He told Angela to put the engine in neutral so he could speak with the man.

"Don't shoot me," the man said. "I ain't done nothing to you."

He lowered the Saiga.

"How did you get here?" Stephen asked.

He told them he was from New Orleans. He had fled the city by boat. He went across the lake, following the ruined bridge. Sections had collapsed when some barges got loose and were driven by hurricane-force winds against it.

"These men come up in a big inboard and took my water, food and gas," he said. "Then they shot my little boat full of holes while I was in it and told me to swim for it."

He explained how, when he was at the end of his strength and thought surely he was going to drown, he came upon a big chunk of Styrofoam. He was able to use that as a life preserver until it broke apart beneath his weight.

"I climbed right up on this limb," he said.

"Why did you leave New Orleans?" Stephen asked.

"Because it's full of water," he said. "The levees broke. Most of the people are gone. The National Guard has pulled out."

Stephen asked him what he thought the area around Audubon Park might be like.

"I imagine it's under about twenty feet of water," he said. "But I don't know. I never had a reason to go there. That's where rich people live. Besides, it's foolish talking about high places. There's no high ground in New Orleans."

If the man was telling the truth, it confirmed what he had heard on the radio. Perhaps he should be more inclined to trust what he heard from the mystery station.

Stephen considered what he should do. One thing was certain—going across the lake would be dangerous. On a day when the lake was perfectly smooth, they would probably be able to outrun many boats. But he could not count on that.

"Boy, are you gonna leave me up in this tree?" the man said.

"Where do you want to go?" he asked.

"A dry place," he said.

"Us too," he said. "Come aboard."

He did not know how Angela felt, but he just could not leave the man in the tree to die.

Stephen expected him to climb out along the limb to where it trailed off into the water. Instead he simply dropped out of the tree. He swam to the boat, and Stephen helped him climb over the side.

"I thought I was going to be in that tree until Christmas," he said.

After he drank plenty of water, ignoring Stephen's warning about drinking slowly, he told them his name was Byron Williams and that he worked in New Orleans as a bartender.

"When they closed the bar, I should've gotten out," he said. "But I thought I'd just hole up in my apartment.

It's on the third floor. I wasn't counting on those new levees breaking. That damn Corps of Engineers can't build a levee that'll hold."

Stephen decided they would head west through the swamps and flooded farmland toward Baton Rouge and high ground. If they were lucky, they would find Interstate 12 and follow it to Baton Rouge. There he would find out for sure if New Orleans had been completely abandoned. Perhaps his mother was in Baton Rouge.

With Byron in the bow to look for debris, he took a seat in the passenger's seat in front of Angela, the Saiga across his legs. He was glad he had stowed the other weapons away. And he would insist that Angela and he would pull watches and let Byron sleep. Angela would wake him if Byron got up. The first dry ground they came to he was going to drop him off and tell him goodbye.

He set a westerly course by the sun. Sometimes they ran through flooded towns and sometimes through swamps. Late in the afternoon Angela guided the boat up into some flooded timber. Somewhere out to the west was Interstate 55, but he would not be surprised if it was completely underwater. Stephen realized it was going to be hard to find Baton Rouge unless they went all the way to the levee on the Mississippi and followed it down to the city.

Byron insisted on being the cook for their supper of beans and rice.

As he cooked, he began to talk about New Orleans, how everything was underwater. Angela told him Stephen's mother was staying and about the security company who was guarding her house, protecting valuable paintings and furniture.

"She'll really appreciate having you home," Byron said. "Maybe she's there. Maybe she's not. Who's to say how high the water is. We can go take a look. I know the way. I guess if I can escape from New Orleans then I can help you get back in. If I can't get you there, I'll get you to Natchez or Baton Rouge. I *know* Natchez ain't flooded. If it is we need to be on the lookout for Mr. Noah."

"I can get myself home," Stephen said.

He suspected Byron was trying to take over. Perhaps he expected a reward from Stephen's mother.

"I know you can," Bryon said.

"He fixed the motor on this boat," Angela said.

"He's a smart boy, all right," Bryon said.

After they ate, Stephen took the first watch, sitting in the driver's seat with the Saiga across his legs. Angela was under the mosquito netting and Byron, who said he was not sleepy, sat in the bow. Pretty soon they could hear the sound of Angela snoring.

"She's your girlfriend?" Byron asked. "I know she's not your sister from the way you look at her."

"What way is that?" he said.

"Not the way you'd look at your sister."

He told him how he picked her up in the flooded town.

"You got a big heart, boy," Byron said. "A big heart."

Byron asked how old he was, and he lied and told him he was sixteen. He considered telling him about the men he had killed so Byron would be wary of him. But he feared it would sound like a boy's bragging. Better to let Byron underestimate him.

Then Byron spent considerable time telling him about all the women he had had in New Orleans.

"A different one every weekend," he said. "I'll bet you just tear it up with them high school girls."

Stephen shrugged.

"I do okay," he said.

Now Byron had maneuvered him into lying and that made him uncomfortable. The next thing he knew Byron would be pressing him to provide details.

Byron laughed quietly.

"I bet you do," he said.

But then he was back to bragging about his exploits with women.

Stephen wanted to tell him he did not see how Byron had time to tend bar and service all those women. But he kept his mouth shut and pretended he was impressed. Finally, to Stephen's great relief,

Byron crawled under the mosquito netting and went to sleep. Stephen wished he could hear him snoring like Angela, but he told himself that perhaps Byron did not snore.

He did not wake Angela, pulling a triple watch instead. No sound came from Byron. He tried finding the mystery station on the radio again, but there was nothing but static. Finally, when he was reduced to fighting to keep his eyes open, he woke Angela.

"Byron moves, you wake me up," he said.

"We should've left him in the tree," she said. "I don't like the way he looks at me."

Stephen had not been aware Byron had been looking at her in any particular way. If *he* were looking at her in that way, she would know, just like she knew about Byron. After all, even Byron had noticed. He slipped beneath the mosquito netting and lay down with the Saiga. He expected to have difficulty sleeping, but instead he fell immediately asleep.

○ ◑ ◡

When she woke him, he struggled to sit up, the Saiga in his hands.

"It's all right," she whispered to him. "Nothing's wrong."

The rest of the night their watches went smoothly. Once it looked like Bryon was awake, but he was just turning over. Then it was Angela's turn.

"You watch him close," he told her.

"I will," she said.

"Don't you go to sleep."

"I won't."

She put her hand on his arm.

"Don't worry, you can count on me," she said.

He woke to the smell of beans and rice cooking. Byron was doing the cooking, and she was sitting beside him.

"Get up, boy," Byron says. "Let's eat and get out of this damn swamp."

FIVE

They worked their way through a labyrinth of swamps, always moving to the west, navigating as best they could by the position of the sun. He liked the swamps because the water was free of debris in places. Occasionally they hit a fast-moving current of brown water, thick with mud and filled with debris: a rocking chair, plastic containers, an occasional dead body. The currents formed rivers within the swamps. Byron thought the currents were from breaks in the main levee along the Mississippi. Stephen recalled the Swamp Hog on the radio saying that. Another indication that what he said was reliable.

He would not have thought he would get used to dead bodies floating around, but he had. He could tell Angela had too. Sometime he wanted to talk with Angela about his father's warning, to see what she thought he meant. But he felt uncomfortable doing that with Byron around. Mostly he had a view of Byron's back, his T-shirt stained with mud, as he sat there on lookout for a clear path.

He was still being careful with Byron, making sure he always had the Saiga in his hands and that Byron did not start hanging around the place where the guns were stowed. Stephen liked him in the bow, where he had a good view of Bryon's back and the man could not keep track of what he was doing. Byron was not a big man. He was nervous and twitchy.

Byron yearned for a cigarette.

"If I just had me a smoke," he kept saying.

The second night on the airboat Byron showed no signs of going to sleep. Angela immediately went off to sleep. He offered to stand his share of the watches, but Stephen refused. Byron acquiesced.

"You're the captain," he said.

Stephen was surprised he did not argue or protest.

"I don't feel much like sleeping," Byron said.

"Angela and I'll stand the watches."

"She's a good-looking girl."

"I know that."

"Maybe you do. Boys like you sometimes don't appreciate girls the way they should."

"I appreciate her. She's a good driver."

"Well, ain't you the cool one."

Stephen said nothing and pretended to be concerned with adjusting the sling on the Saiga.

Byron crawled under the netting. After only a few minutes, he sat up and threw it off.

"I ain't sleepy."

"Then don't sleep."

Stephen gripped the stock of the Saiga tightly and felt the reassuring weight of the magazine full of shells. He would not sleep until Byron slept.

"I wish I had me a smoke," Byron said.

"You could swim to New Orleans for one," Stephen said.

"I appreciate you pulling me out of that tree, but you're being mighty unfriendly. I'm just trying to do my share."

"The best thing you could do would be to go to sleep."

Byron sprayed more mosquito repellent about his head.

"Want me to spray you?" he asked.

"No, thanks," Stephen said.

"You been thinking about your mama?"

Stephen said nothing.

"She's got them mercenaries taking care of her," Bryon continued. "Pretty lady and her mercenaries."

"How do you know she's pretty?" Stephen asked.

"I expect she is. She ain't an ugly woman, is she?"

"No."

"See, I was right. A boy like you should be paying more attention to what I say."

"I've been listening."

"I'll bet yawl have a safe in that house."

"There's no safe. Just paintings and furniture. It doesn't matter. It's underwater."

"I'd have my money in gold. Wherever she is, she's got mercenaries to guard her gold."

"She has no gold."

Then for a long time Byron was silent as if he were actually contemplating having gold to put in a safe. He lay stretched out on the deck. Stephen wondered if he had dropped off to sleep. Stephen was having a hard time staying awake himself. But then Byron stirred and sat up again.

Stephen had just about made up his mind not to sleep at all this night.

"These mosquitoes are not so bad," Stephen said.

"They're bad enough," Byron said.

He woke Angela for her watch. Byron yawned.

"Maybe I am sleepy," he said.

He crawled back under the netting.

Stephen gave Angela the Saiga.

"I...," she began.

He expected she was going to tell him again that she knew nothing about guns.

"Just hold it across your lap," he whispered in her ear. "Keep your fingers off the trigger. He wakes up or starts to move around, you wake me. Don't wait until he comes out from under that mosquito net."

She said she understood. He crawled under the netting.

In the morning he found himself standing watch and listening to Byron talk about his life as a bartender. Angela was asleep under the netting. Stephen thought he had gotten enough sleep to get himself through the day.

○ ◑ ◒

They were forced to move in a more northerly direction by a stiff current to the west that swept through an impenetrable tangle of underbrush. Logs and trash were caught up in the lower limbs of the trees. It was a dangerous place. He planned to get above the levee break and then, he hoped, with parts of the levee in sight, follow it down to Baton Rouge. There he would search for information about his mother. If it turned out she was still in New Orleans, they would go there. There was also no sign of Interstate 55. It seemed to him they had come far enough west to have crossed it.

They had learned from the radio that Baton Rouge was untouched by the flood. The new levees there were holding. New Orleans had been abandoned.

"Your mama is high and dry with her mercenaries someplace," Byron had said. "Keeping them paintings dry. I'll bet they ain't used to guarding paintings. Won't she be surprised when she sees you."

"I expect she will," Stephen said.

Up ahead he spotted the tops of pine trees through the cypresses. That meant high ground ahead.

Bryon was elated.

"I gonna get myself to the Smokey Mountains," he said. "I don't care if I never see the ocean or the Mississippi River again."

Stephen wondered if he had been listening to the Swamp Hog. Maybe going to Baton Rouge was not a good idea. As they moved toward it, the water would be deeper and the currents perhaps unmanageable. It was hard to decide which way to proceed. Perhaps they could get to Natchez or Jackson, some place on high ground the flood had not touched, and find out about his mother's whereabouts. It seemed to him that the National Guard might know.

Angela worked the airboat through the cypresses. She had become an expert driver in just a few days. Then ahead of them he saw smoke. Somebody was on the ridge.

Since he did not know exactly what they were going to find on the ridge, he elected to proceed cautiously. He decided to arm Bryon and Angela. After he learned from Bryon that he was familiar with rifles, he gave him an AK-47. He gave one to Angela too but with an empty magazine. It had been a mistake not to give her at least one shooting lesson. But just having the rifle in her hands would make people think she knew how to shoot.

"I know you don't trust me," Bryon said. "I can't say I blame you. But you'll see. I ain't forgotten how you took me out of that tree."

They heard people shouting to them. As Angela worked the boat through the trees, the ridge rose above them. Then they saw a group of people standing by the water. A johnboat was pulled up on the bank. It was a family: a man, a woman and two children. The man had a shotgun slung over his shoulder.

"Watch that shotgun," he said to Bryon.

"He tries anything and he's a dead man," Bryon said.

"What's the matter with you," Angela said. "Can't you see it's a family?"

The people were dirty and desperate-looking. The children looked frightened.

"Could you spare some water?" the man asked. "My children are mighty thirsty."

"There's water all around you," Byron said.

"Drinking that swamp water has made us sick," the man said.

"You should walk to a road," Stephen said.

"We can't," the woman said. "There's water all around."

"Then go to the next ridge," Angela said.

"We're out of gas," the man said. "I'm afraid to pole or paddle. There's some tricky currents out in the swamp."

Angela gave the man a canteen. He handed it to his wife who gave it to the children. They took great gulps from it until the woman took it away from them.

"My stomach hurts," the boy, who looked like he was eight or nine years old, said.

"Mine too," the girl said.

She was somewhat younger.

The woman flopped down and started to cry, her head between her knees. Her shoulders heaved as she sobbed.

The man, after taking a few careful sips from the canteen, told them how he stayed behind to protect the convenience store he owned. It was on high ground that had never been flooded. Then someone stole their boat, leaving them stranded. The boat pulled up on the bank belonged to his neighbor, now dead.

"Heart attack, I think," the man said.

He explained how the man had come to him for food. As he was getting out of the boat, he collapsed. Then the rising water had driven them out of the store. The family headed north, looking for high ground.

"You sure you didn't murder your neighbor?" Byron asked.

The man's face turned red. "I've never harmed another person," he said.

"But you do agree that boat wouldn't hold another person?" Byron said.

"Yes, but Dexter was dead," the woman said. "We couldn't carry his body around. I'd appreciate it if you'd stop that sort of talk. You're scaring my children."

Stephen told the man he would give him some gas and water and rice and beans.

"Keep heading north," he said. "That's what we're going to do."

He took their gas can from their boat and climbed back into the airboat to fill it from one of the containers. Out of the corner of his eye, he saw Byron moving along the bank. As he turned to see what Byron was up to, automatic rifle fire erupted, the sound rising up and overwhelming everything, making it difficult for him move or think clearly. Angela began to scream. He grabbed the Saiga but slipped and fell backward. Then he struggled to his feet and brought up the shotgun. He intended to catch Byron before he reloaded.

But Byron still had his back to him. He had dropped the empty magazine and was slipping a fresh one into the rifle. The man and his wife and children, alive and hopeful only moments ago, lay sprawled about in grotesque poses. He had a momentary impulse to will them back alive. If he had kept the rifle out of Byron's hands, they would be alive. If he had left Byron in the tree, they would be alive.

Byron turned to him and grinned.

"They won't be needing anything now," he said. "We've got nothing to spare."

Angela was still screaming and had fallen to her knees. He wondered if she had taken a bullet.

"Hush up, girl," Byron said. "You'll see worse before this is over."

Byron was holding the rifle with one hand over his shoulder. Stephen stepped off the bow of the airboat onto the bank. He brought up the shotgun.

"No, don't," Angela screamed.

As she moved toward him, he sidestepped away from her, not wanting his field of fire encumbered.

"Don't!" she said. "Please!"

"Put the rifle down," he said. "I won't ask you again."

Byron bent over and set the rifle on the ground.

"Now step away from it," he said.

Byron backed off a few paces.

"More," he said.

Byron moved far enough away to satisfy him.

"Thank you," Angela said. "Thank you."

"We didn't have food and water for them too," Byron said.

Stephen could tell from the way he said it that he believed he had made a perfectly logical and rational decision.

"You murdered them for no reason," Angela said. "No reason."

Stephen told Angela to go pick up the rifle and to be careful because the safety was likely to be off, the selector switch still set on automatic.

After she retrieved the rifle, he told her to put it in the airboat with the barrel pointing toward the swamp. She did the same with the man's shotgun. He directed Byron to step away a few more yards. Stephen slung his shotgun. While watching him over his shoulder, he pushed the airboat out into the water. He knelt in the bow and told Angela to start the engine.

"Hey, wait," Byron said. "What about me?"

"Don't remind me you're alive," he said.

"What were those people to you?" Byron said.

"They were people," he said.

The engine started, and Angela swung the airboat out into open water. Byron ran up the edge of the water and was screaming something at them, his face all contorted, but Stephen could not make out a word because of the noise of the engine and the propeller.

They went up the side of the ridge, their backs to Byron. Then the ridge swung to the north, and Stephen knew that even if he turned to look in Byron's direction, he would be unable to see him.

The land continued to rise with pine-covered ridges interspersed with cypress swamps. Finally they found their way blocked by a ridge, and after following it for miles to the east, he realized that moving north was not a good idea. Perhaps they should just take their chance with more water and tricky currents. When they hit a creek that flowed to the west, he directed Angela to turn into it. He thought it would be better to try to reach Baton Rouge than to press on north. Late in the afternoon he had her run the boat out of the creek and into a cypress swamp.

They ate and sat in the boat and waited for it to turn dark so they could sleep.

"Why did he kill those people?" she asked.

He liked it that she, a grown woman, was asking him, a boy, a question like that.

"I don't know," he said. "I guess because he could."

"You should've killed him," she said.

He reminded her she was against his doing that and asked her why she changed her mind.

"He gets a chance, he'll kill another family," she said.

He imagined she was thinking of her parents, but he did not say anything.

Then they had a discussion about killing people who are likely to kill innocent people for no particular reason.

"Doing that is another side of anarchy," he said. "But he sure deserved it."

"But you didn't. Why did you pay any attention to me?"

"You sure ask hard questions."

He considered why he had not filled Byron full of buckshot. He thought of the men who killed his father and of the one he let escape. He wondered if he should tell her about that and then he did.

"I've killed enough people," he said. "Let somebody else come along and kill him. I don't want to start deciding who'll live and who'll die."

"I could've killed him," she said. "I just didn't know it at the time."

He told her about his father's observations on the effects of killing and how he did not understand.

"Do you now?" she asked.

"Not really," he said. "Do you?"

"I'm not sure. I think I could kill a hundred Byron Williams and still love the rest of the world." She paused and looked off into the darkness. "Do you think those people your mother hired have had to shoot anyone?"

"I wouldn't be surprised."

"If somebody tried to steal a painting or a fine piece of furniture."

"Or some water or food. All that stuff could be sitting in the house, underwater. Maybe the only thing they could save was themselves."

Byron had called them mercenaries. Stephen supposed that was as good a name for them as any. He wondered if there were four or five of them or just one. By now they could have removed his mother from New Orleans.

"They'd be happy to pull the trigger on somebody," he said.

That was an expression he had heard his father use.

He remembered he needed to teach her to shoot. One problem with that was everyone for miles around would hear the sound. It was something he would do in the morning. He also decided they would not stand watches. She was exhausted and so was he. Both of them could use a good night's sleep. He wondered if she regretted not having the opportunity to pray over the dead family. One thing for sure, if Byron had killed Angela and him, he would not be doing any praying.

"I'm so tired," she said.

They went to sleep. He wrapped his arms around the Saiga.

"Good night," he said.

But she did not reply. She was already asleep. He lay awake for some time, listening to the sounds of the swamp: splashes, night-birds, the rustle of the breeze in the cypresses. There was absolutely no sound to indicate the presence of people. He liked that. His opinion of human beings had been in steep decline, and the experience with Byron took it to the bottom.

He considered getting up and listening to the radio. But he felt too tired to move and too anxious to sleep. Perhaps it was a mistake not to have set a watch. He shifted the Saiga a little to one side, feeling the satisfactory and comforting weight of the box magazine. He smelled the stink of his unwashed body. He told himself over and over they were safe in the darkness of the swamp. Finally he calmed down enough to feel safe closing his eyes. He hoped the sleep that awaited him would be deep and uninterrupted.

SIX

After breakfast, he gave Angela a shooting lesson. He started her out firing one of the AK-47s at a big cypress knee perhaps twenty yards away. Gradually she worked up to a smaller knee at fifty yards. By the time she had shot a hundred rounds, she was hitting most of the targets. He told her for the time being semi-automatic would be fine. He did not like to contemplate the idea of her panicking with the selector switch on automatic. Now anyone who planned on causing them trouble would have to deal with two instead of one. She would no longer be all bluff. He did wonder if she could actually shoot someone.

"You have to use that rifle, you just think about that bartender," he said.

"I will," she said. "I won't let you down."

"I don't want to have to shoot another person. But sometimes there's no choice."

"I don't want to die."

"Me neither."

She chambered a round and then worked the bolt to eject the round from the chamber. She dropped the magazine and then reinserted it and chambered a fresh round.

"See, I could do it blindfolded," she said.

"You're ready," he said.

"Thanks."

He hoped she was ready. He hoped he was never going to have to find out if she was.

After he took his position in the bow, Angela maneuvered the boat out of the swamp and into the flooded creek. They had traveled a mile or so when they came around a bend and saw a barge moored on the slack-water side of the creek. It had a house built on it. Someone had given the house a fresh coat of white paint. It shimmered before his eyes in the sunlight, a stark contrast against the muddy water of the creek and the rusted metal of the barge. A couple, dressed in white bathrobes, were standing at one end of the barge with coffee cups in their hands. First the woman and then the man waved. He waved back. The couple were all smiles. They looked relaxed and peaceful.

"Go in slow," he told Angela.

He settled the Saiga into a comfortable position. As far as he could see, they were not armed. When they got closer, he stood up and slung the shotgun over his shoulder to appear less threatening. Angela steered the airboat up to the side of the barge and put the engine in neutral.

"You the ones doing all the shooting?" the man asked.

"That was us," Stephen said.

"Any trouble?" the woman asked.

They were tall and blond. The woman had long straight hair that fell down her back. The man's hair was long and curly. They were two of the most beautiful people he had ever seen.

"No trouble," he said. "Target practice."

"Target practice?" the man said.

"She's learning to shoot," he said.

"He says I'm already a good shot," Angela said.

"I imagine you are," the woman said.

He wondered if they knew what had been going on in the flooded countryside around them. Surely they had spotted bodies floating down the creek. He wondered if they had a radio. If they had weapons, they were keeping them out of sight.

"Come aboard," the man said.

They climbed aboard. He took the Saiga with him, and Angela her AK-47.

The man's name was Fred, and the woman was Holly. They were locals who had been living on the barge for a year. Holly had a teaching degree from LSU, but she had temporarily taken a break from teaching. Fred did some commercial fishing. A johnboat was moored to the barge with a stack of hoop nets in it. A blue kayak was sitting on the deck at the far end of the barge. They had a garden, now underwater, on a strip of high ground between the creek and the swamp. They had a generator and some solar panels set up on one end of the barge. And a cistern for drinking water. They had recently painted the house and replaced the windows broken by their brushes with the hurricanes.

"We've decided there aren't going to be any more hurricanes," Holly said.

Fred laughed.

"I hope so," he said. "We're out of glass."

Stephen imagined his father would have been pleased with their setup.

"Honey, you can get yourself a shower," Holly said to Angela.

Angela started to cry. Holly put her arm around her, and they walked off into the house together. Angela still had the rifle slung over her shoulder.

He told Fred how Angela and he came to be on the airboat together. Fred had not heard anything of what was going on in New Orleans or Baton Rouge. There was dry land and access to the highway far upstream, but he cautioned Stephen that it was too dangerous to go up there.

"Bunch of drunks with automatic rifles," he said. "I watched 'em through field glasses. They never knew I was there."

"Aren't you worried they'll come down here?" Stephen asked.

"Too much fallen timber in the creek. If you go through the swamp, you have to know the way. We're safe here."

"I hope so."

"You can depend on it."

Fred thought it would be some time before the army started restoring order.

The creek flowed into the Mississippi. They were well north of I-10 and west of I-55. There had been many breaks and overtoppings of the levee, flooding the flat cropland and swamps. They had seen dead bodies of both people and animals in the creek.

"You might could get to Baton Rouge," he said. "But who knows what you're gonna find there. We'd be pleased for you to stay with us until the water goes down. The army will be back in here, and people will have to do right."

Stephen wanted to tell him he was lucky no one had showed up to kill them both and take their water and food. But he said nothing. Fred was a grown man, perhaps thirty or thirty-five years old, and he was just a boy. He would not be eager to listen to a boy's opinions.

"I'll stay for a while," he said. "I don't know about the girl."

"You do what you want," he said. "I know you want to find your mother."

He did want to find her but not necessarily live with her. He just wanted to make sure she was all right.

Holly and Angela came out on the deck. Angela's hair was still wet. She was dressed in some of Holly's clothes.

"I thought she was going to take a shower with that rifle," Holly said.

"You're safe here," Fred said.

Angela looked like she was going to start crying again. He imagined she was thinking of her parents. He supposed he would do the same if he thought too hard about his father. But he also believed he had done all his crying.

He went off to take a shower, leaving the Saiga on deck. He showered with his clothes on before stripping them off and wringing them out. None of Fred's clothes were going to fit him, all of them way too big. He lingered in the shower, feeling the pleasant drum of the hot water against his skin. He began to think of how his father would have been proud of the way he had conducted himself. Even his father could not have prevented Byron from killing the family. Then he found himself thinking of his father lying there on the sand, and he began to weep. He sat down on the floor of the shower and sobbed, his whole body shaking.

Then he tried to focus not on his father's body on the sand but on the grave, colorful fish darting about over it. He seized on this image. Gradually, as he concentrated, he grew calm.

He put on a bathrobe and went back out onto the deck. As he walked through the house, he took a close look at it for the first time. One whole wall was mostly windows, stained-glass ones scattered among the clear panes. There were skylights in the ceiling. It had the feeling of being outside. He liked it that they had found a way to live amid all this chaos in such a beautiful space. But he knew just one random passing of a boat with the wrong people in it, and all of this would disappear.

He went out onto the deck and found them having wine. They offered him some, but he said no. He had had his first glass of wine last Thanksgiving in New Orleans. It was something he did not care for. Then Holly produced a bottle of Coke and ice. They had ice. It had been a long time since he had had a Coke with ice.

As he sat there drinking the Coke slowly and watching the older people drink their wine, he realized that he was quickly slipping back into his status as a boy.

He put his bare foot on the Saiga resting at his feet. And he knew that he was never going to be that boy again, not since the night his father was killed.

At dinner that night he did drink some wine. They had dinner with candles. First it was turtle soup and then wild boar Fred had shot.

"Better than anything you could buy at the store," Fred said.

They all agreed it was.

The table was covered with a white tablecloth. They had cloth napkins. There were several forks and knives for him to choose from. He was glad his mother had taught him what to do. No one mentioned the flooded countryside around them where dead bodies floated. Instead Fred told funny stories about catching big catfish. Stephen did not know if he believed the story about the catfish that towed the johnboat down the creek and wrecked it on a cypress knee. But it was funny, and he laughed along with the others.

That night he was awakened by the sound of music. It was Bach. His mother played it on the piano. He supposed for a moment it was a recording, but then it started and stopped again. He slipped out of his room and followed the music. Holly, dressed in her white bathrobe, was sitting in a dining-room chair, her back to him, playing a cello. He listened for a long time before he went back to sleep. As he lay in bed, he knew he wanted to leave soon. There was no future for them here.

○ ○ ◡

The weather was hot but calm, the sky blue and filled with harmless-looking white clouds. They learned from the radio no hurricanes were wandering about in the Gulf. New Orleans had been totally evacuated, and people had been forbidden to return. Baton Rouge was filled with refugees. For the first time he recalled his mother had friends in Baton Rouge.

He and Fred listened to the radio one night after Angela and Holly had gone to sleep. Without telling Fred, he tried to dial in the mystery station. But for his efforts he was rewarded only with static.

"Nothing much up at that end of the dial," Fred said.

So he tried the Texas station, but that failed to come in too.

"Whose idea was it to live on this barge?" he asked.

"Holly's," Fred said. "We were thinking about building a cabin on a patch of high ground further down the creek. Then she heard about the barge for sale."

Stephen wondered if he could persuade Angela to live with him in his father's house. It could be that the water would go down and the march of the hurricanes cease and the sea rise no further. He could work on motors, just like his father, in the shop. He wondered if Angela would want to go back to the little town if the water went down. He doubted if she could ever stay in the house where her parents were murdered. She might be willing to come live in his father's house. But with a boy like him?

They tried the radio a few more times but then gave up and went to bed. But he found himself unable to sleep. He sat on the edge of his bed in the darkness and searched for stations on the radio. The result was the same: nothing but static. He wondered, if he climbed to the top of one of the big poplars on the creek bank, would that be enough to draw in the mystery station or any station at all? Finally he gave up and went to sleep.

Every day he made sure to keep the Saiga close and listen for sounds of gunshots or motors in the creek. But there was nothing. He did not even hear an airplane fly over. At night he slept in a real bed with the Saiga by his side. Angela was sleeping in another room. He wondered if she slept with the AK-47. He had heard Fred and Holly making love. That made him think of his mother and her young men. It also made him think of Angela. He wondered how many lovers she had had. He wondered how it would feel to put his hands on her.

Because that was something he had never done with any girl, he found it hard to imagine.

At breakfast one morning, Stephen talked about going to Baton Rouge.

"Why not stay here until the army returns," Holly said.

"Yes, then it'll be safe," Fred said.

He told them what he thought, that they had been lucky so far. One day someone was going to come down the creek and kill them.

"My father thought we were safe," Angela said.

"But that was in a town," Fred said. "No one has a reason to come here or even think someone would be living on a barge."

"We came here," he said. "If we were some of those people, you'd be dead."

He imagined Fred and Holly floating facedown in the creek, borne by the steady current toward the Mississippi.

Holly and Fred argued against their leaving for a time but finally gave it up.

Angela wavered about his decision.

"They've got plenty of food," she said.

"Someone can come here at any time and take it," he said.

"The army could come."

"Like I said, anybody could come here and take it."

"You don't trust the army."

"Not when folks are hungry."

She finally agreed that maybe he was right.

○ ◑ ◒

When they left one morning, Fred gave Stephen a six-pack of Cokes.

"You'll have to drink them warm," he said.

"I don't care," he said.

It was not going to be pleasant to return to a diet of rice and beans. But if all went well, they should be in Baton Rouge in a few days.

They headed down the creek. He planned to cross over into the swamp when they got close to the river and then follow the levee down to Baton Rouge. They had traveled two or three miles when he looked back and saw a plume of black smoke against the sky. He told Angela to run the airboat into an eddy next to the bank and cut the engine.

The only sounds were those of the birds. Far off toward the river, he thought he might hear the sound of an airplane. He asked Angela if she heard it, but she said she did not. Angela thought the plume of smoke seemed to be back off toward the pine-covered ridges, not along the creek at all. He wanted to believe that, but he was not so sure.

"Should we go back?" she asked.

"For what?" he said.

He explained that if the smoke was coming from the barge, whoever started the fire might decide to continue on down the creek. They would be better off when they were out of the creek and into the swamp.

Angela lowered her head into her hands and sobbed.

"Those people," she said.

He knew what she meant. They were so beautiful. Amid all the chaos, all the death and suffering, they moved as if some god had placed a magic spell on them.

"Nothing's happened to them," he said.

"What do you mean?" she asked.

"I mean that I think you're right. That smoke is more in the direction of the ridges."

"You don't mean that."

"I do."

But he was thinking of all those windows shattering: blood on bathrobes, white tablecloths floating in the brown water.

"I'm going to believe you," she said. "Don't you be lying to me."

"When have I done that?" he asked.

She had to admit he had not.

"I'm telling no lies now," he said. "But we need to get down this creek and into the swamp."

She started the engine. Before she turned the boat back out into the creek, she looked in the direction of the smoke one more time. It was still thick and black and showed no signs of diminishing. She turned her back to it and concentrated on piloting the boat.

He took up the Saiga, glad talk was now impossible. He was pretty certain they were far enough from the barge so no one could hear the sound of the engine. But he would not relax until they were out of the creek and into the swamp.

SEVEN

They finally found a passage. Once beyond the screen of trees bordering the creek, he saw they were in an enormous flooded field. The river was somewhere off to the west. He looked up at the sun and turned the airboat to the south and Baton Rouge. They ran for several hours. From time to time they came upon dead animals, both wild and domestic, but no humans.

Then up ahead he spotted a tree-covered mound of earth rising out of the submerged field. He had Angela stop the boat while he scanned it with the field glasses. A house was built on the truncated top of the mound. Off in an open space between some pecan trees a helicopter sat.

At any moment he expected to see someone launch a boat from the tiny island to have a look at them or even for the helicopter to venture out. He had Angela stop the airboat.

"The National Guard?" Angela asked.

"Looks like it to me," he said.

The helicopter had military markings. But just because it was a military aircraft did not mean it was in the hands of the military. He expected by now someone on the island was looking at them with field glasses.

"What's that hill?" Angela asked.

"Someone built a house on an Indian mound," he said.

He got out of his seat and took up a position in the bow. He laid the Saiga on the bottom of the boat. He wanted to make it clear to the people on the mound that they had peaceful intentions. No doubt the inhabitants of the mound had food and water to protect.

"Take us in slow," he said.

As they drew closer, he saw two johnboats drawn up on the grass and several people, both men and women standing there looking at them. Two of them waved, and he waved back. Down near the water's edge, the grass was charred black in a band running both ways.

He turned to Angela and motioned for her to go slow.

"Anything happens, give it full throttle," he said. "Run south."

As they drew closer he scanned the people with his field glasses and saw that none of them was armed. They were all dressed in civilian clothes. He would have preferred to see them dressed in National Guard uniforms. Several of them carried long poles to which gigs were fixed. Perhaps they were living on frogs or were spearing fish in the shallow water.

They were only a hundred yards away now. He looked down at the Saiga and rehearsed in his mind how he was going to pick it up if anyone threatened them. He smiled at the people and waved at them. He turned his head and saw Angela doing the same.

Angela ran the bow of the airboat up onto the grass. There were two women, about his mother's age, and three men. One of the women grabbed the bowline. He stepped out of the boat, followed by Angela, and then everyone was talking at once.

"Where did you children come from?" one of the women asked.

So he gave them a quick summary of their journey, how his father was dead and Angela's parents were dead. He mentioned nothing about the men he killed or the murder of the family or of the couple on the barge. He hoped Angela would keep quiet about those matters too.

The people had been plucked off the levee by the National Guard helicopter. After developing engine trouble, it had been forced to land on the mound.

The pilots had given their position but had been told not to expect rescue for a long time. Resources were needed elsewhere, and they were on dry ground.

The refugees were all from some small Mississippi town he had never heard of. One was a banker, another an insurance agent, and the third owned a funeral home. One of the women was married to the banker and the other to the insurance agent. The undertaker had lost his wife in the flood.

"Mr. Parker is beginning to think he made a big mistake staying," the banker said.

Mr. Parker owned the mound and the house on it and the land for miles around. He was determined to ride out the flood just as his ancestors had ridden out previous floods and the Indians before them. The mound was already a large one when the first settlers cleared the land. It had been further enlarged over the years, first with slave labor and then with a bulldozer.

Stephen discovered that the poles and the frog gigs were for snakes. They were having a bad problem with snakes. Mr. Parker had somehow acquired a flame-thrower. He made a circuit of the mound every night and killed snakes. The black band near the water was scorched grass.

"I didn't imagine there were that many snakes in the whole world," the other woman said.

"You had to shoot anybody with that combat shotgun?" the insurance agent asked.

They had moved off from the women and were standing in a group by the bow of the boat.

"No, sir," Stephen said. "Just snakes."

"You can't blame us for asking," the undertaker said. "Looks to me like you're all set to go to war."

"He's got an AK-47," the insurance agent said.

"It's dangerous out there," Angela said.

"I expect it is," the banker said.

Stephen wondered if they were going to be interested in his supplies. Now he wished that he had carried the Saiga ashore. And again perhaps it would have been a good idea to let them know he had killed a few people. But it was too late to start telling stories like that. They would think he was making it all up. To them he was just a boy.

"Let's go find Mr. Parker," the undertaker said. "He'll want to talk to them."

"That helicopter is broke," the insurance agent said. "I don't care what those pilots say about trying to fix it. It's not gonna happen. But it's gonna be tough getting out of here in a johnboat. There's some mean currents and snags out there."

A man wearing knee-high snake-proof boots was approaching. He carried a pole with a gig on the end.

He wore a pistol at his hip. Stephen guessed this was Mr. Parker.

Mr. Parker, like all of them, was dirty and tired-looking. He stopped before them and looked them over, digging the gig from time to time into the soft earth. Then he lifted one of the charred snakes, a big rattler, and tossed it into the water.

He introduced himself and shook both their hands. When Stephen said his name, the man looked at him closely.

"You live in New Orleans?" he asked.

"Yes, sir," Stephen said.

"Over near Audubon Park?"

"Yes, sir," Stephen said.

"Your mother is Anna Hudgins?"

"Yes, sir."

"I know her. She's been to dinner right here. She works with my brother."

He went on to explain that his brother designed Mardi Gras costumes. His wife was one of Stephen's mother's friends. Mrs. Parker was in Baton Rouge.

Stephen told him how he had gone to spend the summer with his father.

"Where's your father?" Mr. Parker asked.

"Dead," Stephen said.

He gave a detailed account of his father's death.

"You killed them with that combat shotgun?" the insurance agent asked.

"No, sir," Stephen said. "Like I said, I was coming back from hunting ducks. It was a Browning."

Then Mr. Parker asked him about his mother.

"She's in New Orleans or maybe Baton Rouge," Stephen said. He explained how she had hired security people to take care of the house and its furnishings.

"Yes, I expect there's been plenty of looting in New Orleans," Mr. Parker said. "Most folks have pretty well given up on that city. Don't you worry about your mother. She'd hire the best."

Then he asked Angela a few questions. She told him how Stephen had rescued her from the flooded town.

"You folks are mighty clean," he said.

Stephen wondered what he was going to say. Angela looked at him.

"Why's that?" Parker asked. "You must have been wandering around these swamps and flooded fields for days."

So he told them about the barge. The moment he said the word *barge*, Mr. Parker interrupted him.

"Fred and Holly are still alive?" Mr. Parker said.

"Yes, sir, they are," Angela said.

"Well, I'm glad you didn't kill them just to get a hot shower," Mr. Parker said.

He laughed at his own joke along with the others.

"I'll like a hot shower," one of the women said. "I want to get to a hotel someplace. A bath would be better than a shower. A long bath."

Stephen wondered exactly how far a person had to go to find that hotel and that bathtub. He expected it would be a long way.

"Stephen, you and Angela come on up to the house," Mr. Parker said. "I'll show you where you'll be sleeping."

"I'll sleep on the boat," Stephen said.

Angela decided she would sleep in the house. He watched her walk off with Mr. Parker.

He went back to the boat and retrieved the Saiga and the radio.

"Worried about snakes?" the insurance agent asked.

"That's right," Stephen said.

"That radio work?" the banker asked.

"Most of the time," Stephen said.

He went up to the house and found that Angela would be sleeping on the screened porch that ran the length of the back of the house. It had begun to grow dark. They were cooking something in an enormous iron pot over a gas grill. It turned out to be a venison chili that Mr. Parker had made. There was corn and beans and squash from his garden.

The pilots and their crew chief appeared. They announced they thought they had repaired the helicopter.

They would be able to fly out in the morning. The refugees were elated.

"We could go to Natchez," the banker's wife said.

"I don't care where we go just as long as it's dry," the insurance agent said.

Stephen cranked the generator and turned on the radio. He found a station out of Baton Rouge. The announcer advised that relief was on the way just as long as another hurricane did not appear.

"What about that station you keep trying?" Angela said.

Stephen wished she had kept quiet about that. He wondered how he would feel if the station came in loud and clear and the Swamp Hog started making those wild statements. He spun the dial and set it on a place where he was sure he would find nothing but static.

"No, that's not the place I mean," Angela said.

She pushed him away and set the dial on the station. To his relief there was just static. Not a single word came out of the speaker.

"I wonder if you dreamed that station," she said.

"You and my father would have gotten along fine," he said. "That's what he told me."

They all ate and watched the sun set over the flooded fields. Mr. Parker hoped the water would go down, and he would be able to plant in a month or so. But he doubted that was going to happen. He expected there would be more hurricanes and more floods and more levee breaks, and pretty soon things would be back to when the Indians inhabited the land and the river spread out over its banks at least once or twice a year, doing whatever it wanted to do.

When it was completely dark, Steven took up the Saiga and the radio and started down to the boat. Mr. Parker offered to go with him. He carried the flamethrower. He wore a gas-powered headlamp.

"Nothing like going out and frying a few snakes after a good dinner," he said.

He followed Mr. Parker down to the water. Halfway down the hill they began to encounter snakes. Mr. Parker left the harmless water snakes alone. He was looking for cottonmouths, rattlers, and copperheads. He held up his hand. Stephen saw a cottonmouth coiled up directly in their path, displaying the white lining of its mouth. Mr. Parker trained the flamethrower on it. He pulled the trigger and the flame leaped out at the snake with a *whoosh*, illuminating the night, and Stephen smelled a gasoline stink. He imagined he could hear the snake sizzling like a sausage on a grill. Mr. Parker played his light over the charred remains.

"The way it's gotten so hot all the time, pretty soon I'll be killing cobras and pythons," he said. "They were starting to have a serious problem in Florida.

Now that Florida's gone, I expect they'll eventually move up this way."

He incinerated a few more cottonmouths and a big rattler on the way to the airboat. Stephen climbed on board.

"Worried about your boat?" Mr. Parker said.

"It's been on my mind," Stephen said.

"Well, I don't blame you. But those folks'll fly out on that helicopter in the morning."

"That suits me just fine."

"You know, I wouldn't be ashamed to have my sons grow up like you."

Stephen did not know what to say. He supposed the sons were in Baton Rouge with Mr. Parker's wife.

"I'm not grown up," he said.

"Oh, I think you've gone as far as it's possible to go," Mr. Parker said.

Stephen wondered what he meant.

Mr. Parker played his light over the grass. It illuminated a couple of small gators, their eyes shining red in the light. There were plenty of snakes.

"Do you think my mother is all right?" Stephen asked.

"She'd hire good people," Mr. Parker said. "If I had a couple of them here, I'd sleep like a baby."

Stephen wondered if Mr. Parker knew about his mother's young men and, if he did, what he thought about it.

"Do you see my mother often?" Stephen asked.

"Now and then," Mr. Parker said. "Courtland would bring her out here for dinner. We had dinner in New Orleans a couple of times."

Mr. Parker adjusted the harness on the flame-thrower tank and settled it more comfortably on his shoulders.

"Josephine still works for your mother?" he asked.

"I guess," Stephen said.

"She is one good-looking woman. I wonder if she's gone back to Lake Charles or is sticking it out with your mother. I expect Lakes Charles is underwater too."

"I don't know."

"No way you could know. Well, I guess I'll take a stroll around the property."

He settled the tank on his shoulders one last time and walked off along the bank. From time to time a stream of flame shot out.

Stephen set up the mosquito netting and then climbed under it, along with the Saiga and the radio. He gave the generator another good cranking and tried to find the mystery station. To his surprise the Swamp Hog's voice came out of the speakers, riding the air over the flooded land.

"*Hello, all of you in Memphis,*" the voice was saying. "*You're on high ground. Stay there. Fish are swimming in New Orleans and Charleston. The land is shrinking, the temperature is rising. Beware of low ground. Hello, there in…"*

Then the voice disappeared in a hiss and crackle of static.

"What about Baton Rouge?" Stephen asked. "What about my mother?"

He tried adjusting the dial, but the only reply was more static.

"Hello, hel…," the voice said.

But then it was gone. He felt like tossing the radio into the water.

"Who are you?" he asked.

His only reply was static.

He turned off the radio and wrapped his arms around the Saiga and tried to sleep. Periodically he heard the *whoosh* of the flamethrower. He could not sleep. He tried to clear his mind of the voice on the radio.

Hello, Hello, Hello.

The voice went on and on in his head.

Finally he slept. But it seemed to him that he had barely closed his eyes when he was awakened by the *whoosh* of the flamethrower. Mr. Parker had made a circuit of the island and was approaching. The flame leaped out, like the breath of some fairy-tale dragon. Mr. Parker played the light over the airboat. Stephen gave up on sleep and sat up under the netting, awaiting his arrival.

The last blast from the flamethrower incinerated something just off the bow of the airboat. Stephen felt the heat of it. He took a deep breath as his lungs searched for oxygen the flame had consumed. Mr. Parker was laughing, a deep rich laugh.

"Boy, are you awake?" he shouted.

Stephen did not reply.

A stream of fire shot out again, this time over the water, followed by the same laughter.

"Wake up, Stephen, wake up!" he shouted.

As Mr. Parker played the light over the airboat, Stephen shielded his eyes against the glare with one hand.

"You be careful with that thing," Stephen shouted.

"It's a lullaby for you," Mr. Parker said.

This time he was close enough he did not have to shout. But he came no closer and turned and walked back up the hill to the house, the flame now and then leaping out from the machine.

EIGHT

Stephen woke at first light. A banded water snake was draped across the bow of the boat, but it dropped off into the water with a solid splash when he moved. The sun was rising on the other side of the mound, while his side was still in shadow. He heard the sound of the helicopter's engine starting.

As he started to pack up the mosquito netting, he stood and waited for the helicopter to rise above the pecans. Finally it did and flew directly over him. He waved to it. One of the pilots waved back. Then suddenly it tilted downward and flew directly into the water only a few yards away. There was no fire, no explosion, just the *thump* of the body of the chopper against the water. The water it threw up rained down on him.

The wreckage floated for a few minutes and then slowly sank out of sight, leaving just a piece of the tail rotor above the water. Just then the sun rose over the trees on the top of the mound and illuminated the wreckage, the light glinting off the metal blades.

Then it occurred to him that Angela might have decided to go with them. He scrambled out of the boat and had started up the hill when he saw Mr. Parker and Angela running down it.

When they reached him, he threw his arms around her. He told her he thought she might have been on the helicopter. And he wondered if his concern was a sign of love. He supposed it could be. But a girl as old as she was would be unobtainable for him. He wondered how many people you had to kill before you could no longer love. Was it a different number for different people?

"Those poor people," she said, looking out toward the wreck. "They thought they were going to sleep in a hotel tonight." Then she turned back to him. "We started out together. We're going to stay together until we get to Baton Rouge."

Mr. Parker stood at the edge of the water, weeping.

"God, they're all gone," Mr. Parker said.

Stephen noticed something floating in the water that looked like a piece of a body, but he said nothing.

"I cooked breakfast for them," Mr. Parker said. "How can they be dead?"

Angela put her arms around Mr. Parker, and Stephen joined her.

Mr. Parker was making Stephen feel old. Stephen recalled running his hands over his father's body. They were dead; they were not alive. It was as simple as that. He wondered if he had now grown older than his mother and Josephine. What had they seen in New Orleans? Those security men, although young, were probably the oldest people he was likely to meet. They, and men like them, had traveled the furthest from life.

His father had obviously been one of them, but now it was too late to learn any of his hard-earned wisdom.

Angela began to cry too, but she was comforting Mr. Parker, telling him they did not suffer, that it was quick. Stephen found he could not weep for them. His mind was filled with the sound of those cries of the wounded man the night his father was killed. He had definitely decided the cries had not come from his father.

She was telling Mr. Parker they were all gone to Jesus, and he was saying that was true.

Stephen still could not focus his attention on the dead. He was studying what he was feeling for Angela. But he did not think there was any hope for him. He supposed she regarded him as her little brother. It was not like his mother and her young men.

Mr. Parker sat in the mud by the side of the water. The sun shone brightly on the now perfectly calm brown water. Stephen walked over and put his hand on his shoulder.

"Let's go up to the house, Mr. Parker," he said. "We can make some coffee."

They turned their backs on the wreck and went up the hill. Stephen was going to suggest they have coffee on the porch. Stephen made the coffee. They all sat and looked out on the flooded land.

"You'll be going to Baton Rouge today?" Mr. Parker asked.

"Yes, sir," he said.

Mr. Parker asked them again if they had his wife's address in a safe place. Angela had memorized it and recited it to him. He seemed to be satisfied.

Stephen wondered how he was going to feel being alone again.

"You can come with us," Stephen said. "You can use the airboat to come back."

Mr. Parker thanked him for his offer but said he'd rather stay.

"I've got property to protect," he said. "I don't want to come home and find looters have been at this house. They could burn it down just for fun, you know."

Both Stephen and Angela told him they understood about that. Then he went off to check on the generator he was using to run a freezer.

"We can't go today," Angela said.

"Why not?" Stephen asked.

"And leave him here all alone?"

"He could come with us."

"Didn't you see him when the helicopter crashed. It's more than just those people dying. He's unsettled."

"You mean crazy?"

"No, but look what's happened to his land. And going around at night with that flamethrower after snakes. Why, one man couldn't make a dent in them. There're millions more out in that water."

So when Mr. Parker returned, they told him they would be staying a few more days.

"If that's all right with you," Angela said.

Mr. Parker seemed pleased.

"Sure, stay as long as you want," he said. "But if Anna is in Baton Rouge, you need to go there. You know she's worried about you."

Stephen pointed out he had been gone all summer.

"She can wait a few more days," he said.

"I can't say I won't appreciate your company," Mr. Parker said.

The rest of the day Stephen spent listening to the radio. There were the usual conflicting reports. The water was rising. The water was going down. Nothing but static when he turned the dial to the mystery station.

After they ate dinner and it grew dark, Mr. Parker went out and used the flamethrower on a few snakes that had crawled up near the house. But he took Angela's suggestion to leave those near the water alone.

Mr. Parker went to sleep early at one end of the porch. It had grown too hot at night to sleep in any of the bedrooms. Stephen and Angela sat there in the dark. Now and then splashes came up from the water. A gator grunted.

Stephen wondered what it would be like to lie with her on the mattress. He wondered how many lovers she had had. She was telling him about a trip she had taken the summer before to visit a friend in the North Carolina mountains.

"The water won't come up to those mountains," she said.

"Did it rain all summer?" he asked.

"No, it was hot and dry."

"I wonder if it's raining there now?"

"You could try the radio."

"I've never heard anything about those mountains on the radio."

He decided not to tell her about the Swamp Hog's talk of the Rocky Mountains covered with jungle.

Then he thought about both of them sitting there naked.

"Stephen?"

"What?"

"Are you thinking about your mother?"

"Yeah, I guess I am."

He felt a little strange and uncomfortable telling that lie.

"Maybe we'll find her in Baton Rouge. We'll be there in a few days."

Stephen wondered if she believed that. He was not sure what to believe himself. It was taking them a long time to get to Baton Rouge. As for his mother, he would not be surprised to learn she and those security people were the only people, besides a few over-optimistic looters, in New Orleans.

She said she was going to sleep.

"Mr. Parker is going to rig up a shower tomorrow," she said. "And he's going to let me have some of his wife's clothes."

Stephen lay down to sleep. From the other end of the porch came the regular sound of Angela's breathing. He found himself lying there and thinking not about Angela but the safety of the airboat. Although he had the keys in his pocket, someone who knew what he was doing could find a way to start the engine. Tomorrow he would disable the distributor. Then he was sure he would sleep soundly.

In the morning he woke at first light, and taking up the Saiga and one of the gigs, he went down to the airboat. There was a thick fog lying on the surface of the flooded field, but he could see the ground before him clearly. He prodded several snakes out of his path with the pole.

He was relieved to see the airboat exactly where he had left it. The piece of the tail rotor had vanished beneath the brown water. The water was on the rise. It was filled with trash. And there was a current, bearing trash and dead animals and then one, two, three and perhaps a fourth body off to the southwest.

Angela was calling his name. He shouted out to her that he was coming up the hill. He would do something about disabling the airboat after breakfast. As he neared the house, Angela came out to meet him.

"The water's rising," he said. He told her that the wreckage of the helicopter had vanished.

"Try your radio and let's see what's happening," she said.

So before breakfast they all sat on the porch and listened to several contradictory reports. He did not try the mystery station.

Mr. Parker was disgusted.

"Next thing you know they'll be telling us that it's all the result of the snow melting off the bluff at Memphis," he said.

"Some levee or dam broke someplace," Stephen said. "Or maybe it's more rain upstream."

"I'm just glad we don't have to look at that helicopter," Angela said.

Stephen thought that he was glad they did not have to look at the bodies from the wreck. But he said nothing. He turned off the radio.

"I'm hungry," he said. "Let's eat."

"God, I wish I could have some scrambled eggs," Angela said.

"How about pancakes and blackberries," Mr. Parker said. "I've got some of Sally's in the freezer. I picked the blackberries."

Stephen tried to imagine what Mr. Parker's wife Sally looked like. He imagined her in the kitchen making the pancakes and looking out across the fields of soybeans or corn that stretched to the horizon. It seemed strange to him that people might die, as those in the helicopter had, and the survivors might mourn, but pretty quickly folks got interested in eating and drinking again.

He stood up and walked to the edge of the screen so he might have a good view of the flooded fields. The brown water glittered in the sunlight as a morning breeze stirred its surface. He tried to imagine the field lush and green with beans and cotton.

NINE

They were having lunch on the porch when Angela spotted something far off on the flooded field near the tree line marking the edge of a swamp. It was blue and moving across the open water toward them.

"It's a canoe or a kayak," Angela said.

He picked up the field glasses and took a look.

"It's a kayak," he said.

They all took a turn with the glasses. The kayak came on straight toward them. Stephen could for the first time see the paddler clearly through the glasses. Her long blond hair was tied back in a ponytail under a baseball cap.

"It's Holly," he said.

It was if he was witnessing some act of magic, the dead raised before his eyes. The only thing better would be to see his father come paddling out of the trees. But finding his mother could turn out to be just the same. He imagined taking the airboat to Baton Rouge and there she would be, standing on the levee, as if she were keeping an appointment to meet him. Perhaps his problems with her had been his fault. After all, she had the right to a private life. Once he found her, he was determined to conceal his disdain for those young men. But he would not be unhappy if she sent him off to school. She would be easier to deal with if he just saw her at Christmas and Thanksgiving. Maybe in the summer he could go stay in his father's house.

Mr. Parker asked for the glasses.

"Yes, that's her," Mr. Parker said.

They all went down to where the airboat was moored to await her arrival.

When she was several hundred yards away, she stopped paddling.

"What's she doing?" Angela asked.

"Looking us over," Stephen said.

"Yes, it's what I'd do," Mr. Parker said.

Angela began to wave her arms and yell out Holly's name.

"I told you that smoke was off in the wrong direction to be the barge," she said.

Stephen shrugged.

"I hope you're right," he said.

Holly still sat motionless in the kayak, her hair bright in the sunlight. She took up the paddle and dipped it into the water. As she lifted it, a shower of golden drops trailed after the blade.

Now Stephen and Mr. Parker began to wave their arms too and call out her name.

She finally waved back and took up the paddle and swung the bow of the kayak toward them.

"Come on!" Angela yelled. "Come on!"

Stephen and Mr. Parker joined her.

Holly stopped paddling. The kayak, caught by a slight breeze, swung in a slow circle.

"Stephen, if she doesn't come in, you take the airboat out to her," Angela said.

"I think she'll come in," Stephen said.

He was wondering where Fred was. Perhaps off fishing in the johnboat.

Holly took up the paddle again and, obviously having made up her mind, she paddled hard toward them.

Soon she was standing beside them, hugging Angela. She handed out hugs to Stephen and Mr. Parker. Then she abruptly sat down on the charred grass. She began to alternately laugh and weep, and then, it seemed to Stephen, she was doing both at the same time.

"I never expected to find you two here," she said. "I came to see if William was sticking it out. I knew he would be."

Her face was wet with tears.

"Where's Fred?" Mr. Parker asked.

"Oh, William, I don't know," she wailed.

Mr. Parker reached down and helped her to her feet.

"You come on up to the house," he said. "Have something to eat, maybe a drink. Then you can tell us all about it."

○ ◐ ◑

Back at the house she stood at the screen and looked out over the flooded fields.

"The water keeps rising," she said.

"It'll go down," Mr. Parker said.

He made her and Angela drinks. Stephen got his last Coke from the refrigerator.

Holly sat and sipped her drink and told them how she was in the kitchen cooking when Fred came running into the room with a deer rifle in his hands. At the same moment, she heard automatic gunfire, and the windows of the house fragmented. Stephen imagined the fragments tinkling as they fell, a heavy rain of glass, onto the steel deck. Then there was an explosion that shook the entire barge. She heard Fred shooting the deer rifle, the sound of it filling the small space.

"The kayak!" he had yelled. "Quickly!"

"Where?" she had asked.

"Into the swamp."

She told them how she wanted to stay, but he pushed her out the back door. He pointed to the swamp.

"You hide," he said. "I'll come get you."

She took the kayak down the creek, her escape shielded from view by the end of the barge. She worked her way along the creek bank for perhaps half a mile until she came to a canebrake. She paddled deep inside it, forcing the boat between the canes until she was completely concealed from the creek.

"Then it caught on fire, and the shooting stopped," she said. "But Fred never came for me."

Stephen imagined her sitting there in the cane, listening to the birds sing. She might have found the silence more threatening than the sounds of the shooting. Because she had no way of knowing if Fred were dead or alive, all she could do was wait.

They all offered opinions as to what had happened to Fred. Like the others, Stephen invented an optimistic outcome, but he was certain Fred had been killed. What chance did a man with a deer rifle stand against people with automatic weapons? He was going to be happy when they were on the airboat again. The house was a tempting target.

Or, he thought, was this fatalistic view part of what his father had warned him about? Was he going to be condemned the rest his life to see things painted in only one shade?

She described going back to the charred remains of the house after spending the night in the canebrake. The johnboat was gone.

It could be the same with his mother. He imagined riding in the bow of the airboat and Angela turning it onto their street. On either side would be the charred remains of big houses, burned down to the water that surrounded them.

In a metal storage shed at one end of the barge, Holly found fishing gear, a gas camping stove and a little fuel. Under camouflage material for a duck blind, a case of bottled water. The people who burned the house had probably been in too much of a hurry to search carefully or decided that what they found in the shed was not worth stealing.

She set off back up the creek, intending to go through the swamp to Mr. Parker's house. That had taken her much longer than she had thought, especially after the water started to rise. She had had to struggle with strong currents in places. She had wandered about the swamp for several days until, almost out of water, she had paddled out into the flooded field.

She asked Stephen if he would use the airboat to search for Fred. He said he would, not having the least idea where they should start. There was nothing to be gained by going back to the barge. But she seemed relieved he was willing to try.

"We have a plan," she said.

She continued to repeat the words under her breath, like a sort of prayer.

Stephen decided to suggest they look for Fred in the direction of Baton Rouge. It was logical he might have headed that way in the johnboat. He did not want her to start wondering why Fred never returned to look for her. He would have expected her to know better, she being a grown-up, but her good judgment had been twisted by the violent events she had endured. He was glad that had not happened to him. He thought he still saw things clearly.

As they continued to drink, Holly and Mr. Parker began to tell stories about Fred. He had dropped out of high school to be a commercial fisherman. Some universities had been interested in him as a football player.

"He always said he'd rather fish than play football," Holly said.

"If he'd played, he'd have been a good one," Mr. Parker said.

"Those coaches would come to his mamma's house. All they got out of it was a good meal," Holly said.

Stephen wanted to wave his arms and implore them to stop.

Can't they see he's dead? he thought.

And he wondered if Angela was thinking the same thing. She had clung to the hope the smoke was from some other source. He wished his father was here. He would make them stop and then explain in kind but direct language that Fred had been killed. One man with a deer rifle against people with automatic weapons. The outcome was obvious. Stephen recalled that his father, experienced in combat, had stood no chance at all.

"He's out there someplace," Mr. Parker said. "Catching big catfish and probably having a fine time."

Stephen felt uncomfortable. He looked at Angela, who appeared to have found something interesting on the floor between her feet.

"If they killed him, I'd have found him," Holly said.

Stephen wondered if the sort of fire that had occurred could consume a human being completely. Fred's killers would not have bothered to bury him or even to toss his body off the barge and into the creek. It now was clear to him that both Mr. Parker and Holly were being foolish in some sort of grievous way that was going to entangle them all in a futile search for Fred.

"He's out there," Mr. Parker said.

"There's miles and miles of flooded timber and fields," Stephen said. "It won't be easy."

"We'll start with the barge," Mr. Parker said. "He could have gone back there by now, looking for Holly."

Stephen agreed to use the airboat the next day to go take a look at the barge. He tried to let himself be seduced by their optimism. He imagined rounding the bend in the creek and there would be Fred standing on the deck of the burned-out barge. Perhaps he had pitched a tent on the barge or built a lean-to.

He went off to bed, leaving Mr. Parker and Holly to talk about Fred, and Angela to listen. As he drifted off to sleep, he caught snatches of their conversation. Angela was worried about returning to the barge. Holly and Mr. Parker were trying to reassure her.

Stephen wondered if this was Angela's way of dissuading them from making the foolish search for Fred. He lay stretched out on the mattress someone had dragged onto the porch from one of the bedrooms and tried to imagine what finding Fred at the barge would be like.

First they would smell coffee. Then they would see Fred standing there, a coffee cup in his hand. Charred remains of the house would be scattered about on the deck of the barge. Fred's face would be black with soot from the fire.

"Let me tell you about this big catfish," he would begin.

And then he would tell a story about being towed up the Mississippi to Natchez by an enormous catfish as big as a whale.

Stephen thought he heard a train whistle off in the distance. But that could not be so because the tracks were underwater. He closed his eyes and imagined Fred hopping a freight.

Holly laughed at something and the others joined in, drawing him out of the dream.

As he finally drifted off to sleep, he remembered he had done nothing about disabling the distributor. At least he had carried all the provisions, including the extra gasoline, up to the house.

"All the way to Covington," Holly was saying.

He could make no sense of that as he dropped into sleep.

TEN

After breakfast they all started down to the airboat. They carried gas, water, food and plenty of ammunition. As they reached the shoulder of the hill and the view of the flooded fields below presented itself, Stephen saw the airboat was gone. In its place was a wooden skiff. In the skiff was one paddle, but no outboard was attached. The skiff was partially filled with water. Someone had made a bailer out of a half-gallon milk jug by cutting off the bottom.

"Had to paddle and bail at the same time," Mr. Parker said.

Stephen pointed out to the others he did not believe the thief or thieves would get far. There was only a little gas in the tank. He scanned the flooded fields with the glasses, but there was no sign of the airboat.

Mr. Parker offered Stephen the use of one of his johnboats. He and Holly would stay and guard the house. They would have to postpone their trip to the barge until Stephen returned.

"You think you can handle that thief?" Mr. Parker asked Stephen.

"Yes, sir, I do," Stephen said.

"It sure looks like it was one person," Mr. Parker said. "If there'd been two, they'd have made another paddle out of a board. There's plenty of lumber floating around. Don't you take chances with him. Kill him. Get your boat back."

"Yes, sir, I will," Stephen said.

He realized that Mr. Parker was right. He should take no chances with the thief.

"Do what your daddy would've done," Angela said.

"He would've disabled the motor and that airboat would still be sitting right here," Stephen said.

They all laughed.

"But he won't get far," Stephen said. "There wasn't much gas in the tank."

Now the task of carrying the heavy cans up the hill was worth it. His father would have been proud of that.

Once they had loaded the johnboat, they set out across the flooded field. Angela ran the motor, and Stephen sat in the bow with the field glasses and the Saiga.

He spotted a few alligators with the glasses, but there was no sign of the airboat. He had Angela run the boat slowly along the edge of the swamp, thinking that the thief might have run the boat up into the cypresses.

"We're lucky he didn't come up to the house and kill us all while we slept," Stephen said.

Angela sat in the stern with the motor, a grim look on her face.

Not having a watch had bothered him from the first night, but he had deferred to Mr. Parker and the rest of the adults.

"No use getting a good night's sleep if you wake up dead," Stephen continued.

"I know you'd have liked to set a watch," she said.

He wanted to tell her they wouldn't be out here right now if they had, but he kept his thoughts to himself.

Then he noticed a broken sapling. The break looked fresh to him. They had done that too as they maneuvered the airboat in tight places in a swamp. He asked her to take the boat into the trees.

She eased it through the trees, now and then banging the hull against a cypress knee or a tree. They heard the airboat engine. He had her cut the motor.

The big engine started and sputtered and went silent. He would not have thought that the thief had run out of gas quite so soon. Then the engine started, and they heard the thief maneuvering the boat through the trees. He would have heard the sound of their motor too. Stephen scanned the trees ahead with the field glasses.

Gradually the trees thinned, and they came out into an open space and moving water. The johnboat shuddered a little as the current caught them up and bore them downstream, the channel running straight through the cypresses. Up ahead, several hundred yards away, he saw the airboat. The engine was running rough, the boat turned sideways in the current. It was going to be easy to catch up with it. A single figure was in the boat.

The airboat made a sudden turn to the left and disappeared into the trees. When they reached the spot, he saw it had encountered an even swifter current. He realized the turn had not been a voluntary one. He turned to warn Angela, but it was too late. The current seized the johnboat and jerked it to one side.

Ahead he saw a chute, the water hissing as it slid between the trees, and at the bottom was a smooth, glasslike standing wave. The wave had caught the airboat and was holding it. As the boat tilted at one angle and then another, the thief tried to maintain a precarious balance.

It was the bartender.

He was yelling something at them. As the wave pitched the airboat up at an angle, he toppled into the water. The airboat shot out of the wave and downstream. Stephen expected to see him emerge, but he did not.

When they hit the wave, the johnboat shuddered and stopped. The propeller whined as it turned in air instead of water. Then it gained purchase again. He looked up at the wave, higher than his head. As the boat climbed the face of the wave, he saw, up in the clear sky, the contrails of some sort of aircraft, flying so high he could not make out the shape of it.

The boat, now half full of water, tilted to one side. He began to bail frantically, using his hat and holding the Saiga with the other hand. Ahead, on the right side of the flow, the airboat was being carried into the trees. It made a crack when it hit them and turned on its side. Then there was a tearing sound as the metal was ripped apart.

He looked back at the wave but saw no sign of Byron Williams in the river below. The motor died. Angela was frantically pulling on the starter rope. The motor started, and she straightened up the boat so it was no longer borne sideways by the current. As he continued to bail, she gradually regained control.

They swung around a bend. He motioned for her to try to steer the boat to the calmer water on the inside of the bend. But the current was too strong. The boat turned sideways again. They both saw the snag coming, a cypress treetop, but it was too late to avoid it. The boat hit it with a thud, the force throwing them both into the bottom of the boat. They were caught fast.

When he picked himself up, he saw a big boat approaching. The olive drab boat looked like a floating rectangular box. Two black men dressed in blue and white uniforms stood in the cockpit. He had seen those uniforms on a TV show about the rodeo held at the state prison every spring. The men were prisoners from Angola.

Their boat did not seem to be affected by the swift current. The pilot slid it up to them, and the other man helped first Angela and then him into the boat. Angela had lost her rifle, but Stephen had the Saiga securely slung across his body. The dry bag containing water, ammo, food and the radio had fallen out of the boat when they encountered the wave. With any luck they should be able to find it, unless it had gotten hung up in underbrush upstream from them.

As the johnboat turned on its side and filled with water, there was that now-familiar sound of metal tearing.

Then the pilot turned the boat, and they went downstream with the current. Stephen realized the boat was a pump jet. The current was no problem for it at all.

As the current gradually diminished, the pilot pulled back on the throttle and ran the boat into an eddy. Stephen unslung the Saiga and held it casually at his side. He saw no weapons in the boat.

The dry bag had ended up in the same eddy. The pilot maneuvered the boat so that Angela could retrieve the bag. Then he saw the body of Byron Williams floating facedown. The prisoners paid no attention to him. Neither did Angela. He thought about telling them the dead man had stolen their airboat, but he did not think it would be worth the trouble. Stephen was glad that the water had done the killing and not him.

"What are you children doing out here?" the pilot asked.

Stephen guessed the pilot was in his forties. The other man was much younger. They were Richard and Drexel.

"Trying to get to Baton Rouge," Stephen said.

He was going to be careful not to mention his mother's house in New Orleans or her hiring of security men. That had caused problems with Byron Williams. He did not want the prisoners to start looking on him as someone who could be a ransom opportunity.

"This water's rising, and pretty soon there'll be catfish swimming in the mayor's office," Drexel said.

"We think we're north of interstate twelve and west of fifty-five."

"You don't know that," Richard said. "Those interstates are underwater."

"I know it's rising," Drexel said.

Richard told them he was serving a life sentence for killing his wife.

"I didn't mean to," Richard said. "I put my hands on her, and then she was lying there. It didn't seem real at all. You know what I mean?"

Drexel was serving a long sentence for armed robbery.

"Might as well be life," Drexel said. "No parole. I'll be ninety years old when I get out." He paused and looked up at the sky as if he were pondering something.

"What's that Mississippi song?" he said. "Let's see. It's about Parchman Prison. 'I'm gonna be here for the rest of my life/And all I did was shoot my wife.'" They all laughed. "But that's about Richard, not me. I didn't shoot nobody. I had a pistol, but I wasn't planning on using it. The jury didn't believe me. That DA said I was a killer. But what about all those other banks I robbed? I didn't hurt a single person. Just scared 'em."

"I ain't from Mississippi," Richard said.

"Well, that song's about you anyway," Drexel said.

Stephen was surprised by how matter-of-fact they were about their crimes.

They were looking for someone to surrender to. They had volunteered to help the Corps of Engineers. When the levee they were working on had failed, they became separated from the engineers and had used the boat to save themselves.

"This is an army bridge erection boat," Richard said. "That chute was no problem for it."

"We've been going around looking for folks to save," Drexel said. "But I don't imagine there's nobody left to save. Just the dead floating about."

"I like the dead to stay put," Richard said. "In the ground, where they belong."

"We're hoping maybe the governor will give us a pardon for bringing the boat back," Drexel said.

"They'll say we stole it," Richard said.

He turned to Stephen.

"You can put that shotgun down," Richard said. "I ain't got any more killing in me. Drexel won't be making anymore illegal withdrawals. Just tell the police we saved you."

"There's no pardon in showing up with a boat full of dead folks," Drexel said.

Stephen hoped they were telling him the truth. He planned to keep the Saiga close by and to make sure that either he or Angela was awake at all times.

"Take us to Baton Rouge," Angela said.

"Not possible," Richard said. "This water's rising. We'll go to Natchez."

The prisoners began to discuss the best way to get to Natchez. They finally decided to find the levee and follow it north to high ground.

That night, the boat anchored in the calm waters of a swamp, Stephen got the radio out of the dry bag and dialed in a few stations. They learned the Mississippi was still rising and more levees were breaking.

The prisoners discussed the breeches in the levees. Richard thought that would relieve the pressure on the levees from the rising river as more water spread out into the fields. Drexel held the opposite opinion.

"See about the mystery station?" Angela asked.

So Stephen dialed it up, and to his surprise it came in loud and clear.

"*This is the Swamp Hog,*" the voice said.

The prisoners started to laugh.

Richard explained that the Swamp Hog was the name of a prison disk jockey. The prison had a small radio station. Drexel wondered how the signal was going this far.

"Besides, that station is underwater now," Richard said.

"He's found himself another transmitter," Drexel said.

"I wonder where that is?" Richard said.

"Someplace dry," Drexel said.

"Maybe on high ground in Mississippi," Stephen said.

"Duck Hill," Drexel said. "I used to live near there. It's got that hill that's mostly rock right beside the railroad tracks."

"There ain't no transmitter on the top of Duck Hill," Richard said.

"I'm not sure that's what they call that hill," Drexel said. "Maybe Snake Hill. There're lots of snakes on it."

"He don't know what he's talking about," Richard said.

It turned out that the Swamp Hog was known to be a little crazy.

"I wouldn't believe nothing that crazy man says," Richard said.

Drexel agreed.

"He uses words he don't know the meaning of ever since that lady from the university taught him to write poetry."

The Swamp Hog was going on about how there was nothing left of New Orleans but the tops of the buildings (he called it the French Quarter Archipelago) when static broke in, and they lost his signal.

Drexel picked up the radio.

"Hey, Swamp Hog," he said. "Where you broad-casting from? Hey, you listening to me?"

When they went to sleep, Stephen did not bother to set watches with Angela. But he did sleep with the Saiga and make sure a round was in the chamber.

ELEVEN

They worked their way through the flooded fields and swamps. The boat handled the swift currents from levee breaks with no problem. Stephen wondered if they would by chance pass by Mr. Parker's house on the mound, but they never saw it, although they passed over many immense flooded fields.

Richard and Drexel were worried about running low on diesel fuel. They had only two drums left.

"That high ground is only a day away," Richard said.

"What does he know?" Drexel said. "We could be a week from Natchez."

"Why, I could get us to St. Louis in a week," Richard said.

"On two drums?" Drexel said. "You can't get us nowhere on that."

So the banter between the two went on. Stephen could tell that Angela was getting just as tired of it as he was.

The afternoon of the third day they came out of a swamp and into a flooded field. In the center of the field was a nineteenth-century riverboat, complete with smokestacks, paddlewheel and plenty of ginger-bread on the pilothouse. It had tilted slightly to one side.

"Come to rest on a mud bank," Richard said.

Richard put the engines in neutral as they all looked at the incongruous scene.

"One of them gambling boats," Richard said.

Richard suspected it could have been moored at Natchez or Vicksburg and been torn loose by the rising river.

"I wouldn't have thought one of them fake things could float long enough to get way down here," Drexel said.

"Looks real to me," Angela said.

"It probably don't even have engines in it," Richard said. "No smoke has ever come out of them smokestacks."

"Then how did it get down the river?" Stephen said.

"You're right," Drexel said. "It should've been smashed into little pieces against that flooded timber."

"God having some fun," Richard said.

"He has a plan," Angela said.

Stephen wanted to point out that it seemed to him that God's plan included plenty of dead people. He almost came out and said that luck, both good and bad, was the same as God.

They decided to spend the night on the riverboat.

"I'll sleep in a bed," Richard said.

Then Drexel started to talk about playing the slots. Richard pointed out he had no money and the machines had no power.

Drexel tossed a rope over a railing and climbed up the side. Everyone went up the rope. They carefully moored the bridge boat to the riverboat with both bow and stern lines.

"What's going to happen if the water rises?" Stephen asked.

"Why should it rise tonight?" Drexel said.

"If it does, it'll just be easier to get back in the boat," Richard said.

Stephen remembered how the wreckage of the helicopter had vanished overnight.

"We've seen it come up fast," Angela said.

But the prisoners were no longer listening. They had wandered off to the big room where the gambling machines were in place. Stephen and Angela followed them. There was rotting food in the serving trays at the buffet in the dining room. Richard and Drexel each helped themselves to a bottle of whiskey from the bar. Then they all had a dinner of army combat rations. Stephen wanted to suggest they stand watches. He did not wish to wake in the morning and find the bridge boat gone.

When it began to grow dark, they all selected a bedroom. Stephen and Angela took bedrooms next to each other.

"Those men are drunk," Angela said.

"They'll go to sleep," Stephen said. "Besides they're looking for a pardon from the governor."

"I don't want to sleep alone."

They decided she would sleep in his room. It was hot in the room. The bed sat at a slight angle.

"That window needs to be opened," she said.

"I'd rather be hot than have mosquitoes," he said.

"Being hot is worse."

She went to the window and searched for a way to open it, only to discover it was the kind you could not open.

Stephen broke a chair and used the leg to smash the glass in the window. He tried to make as much of it as possible fall on the outside.

"We're up high," she said. "Maybe they won't bother us up here."

"In a few minutes you'll see that you're wrong," he said.

Before they went to sleep, he pushed a sofa against the door. He lay down on one side of the bed and she on the other. He put the Saiga between them. He closed his eyes. To his surprise there were no mosquitoes.

"You have the shotgun close?" she asked.

"Yes," he said. "We'll hear someone at the door. They're unarmed. They won't try to come in here."

He slept but was awakened not by mosquitoes but by a thunderstorm passing over them. The boat shook as the thunder boomed. He looked across the bed. She was sitting up.

"Do you hear someone at the door?" she asked.

"It's just the thunder," he said.

She crawled across the bed to him and hit her knee on the Saiga.

"Oh," she said. "You do have it close."

"Careful, there's a round in the chamber," he said.

She picked up the gun. The lightning flashed, and he saw she was pointing it at the door.

"They wouldn't have a chance," he said.

"You think so?" she asked.

"Yes."

"I could do it?"

"Yes."

"Well, I don't know."

"You could if you had to."

"Have you noticed there're no mosquitoes?"

So far she was right about that.

"It's early," he said. "They'll be here."

She put the gun on the bed behind her and lay down beside him.

"Holly thinks we're lovers," she said.

"What did you tell her?" he said.

"That we're not. Not yet."

She sat up and bent over him and kissed him. She tasted of the Tabasco sauce they had all put on their rations to make them palatable.

She slipped out of her clothes.

"You're going to make love with your clothes on?" she asked. "If that's your style, I'll just have to find somebody else."

She laughed and then he did. He slipped off his clothes.

"Have you ever been with a girl?" she asked.

"No," he said.

He had considered lying but decided that she would know somehow, and that would make him look even more foolish.

"What about Jesus?" she asked.

"What about him?" he said.

"I don't know if I could sleep with a boy who doesn't believe in Jesus."

He imagined she thought that his father was in Hell and that was exactly where he was going.

"My father didn't," he said.

"I'm not asking you about your father," she said. "Jesus has been watching out for us. You heard what Richard said about this boat. That it's a miracle it got down the river and into this field."

"He didn't say anything about a miracle."

"Not exactly, but what he said amounts to the same thing. Anyway, I've been praying ever since we met. We're still alive. That's a kind of miracle too."

"I guess you could call it that."

He discovered it was easy for him to be evasive about religion. Besides, it was unfair her holding that over him.

"Just say you do," she said.

"I don't not believe in Jesus," he said.

"What does that mean?" she said.

"That I'm not opposed to the idea of him."

"That makes me so happy."

She reached out and put her hand on him.

"Well, it doesn't look like you're nervous," she said.

She pulled him toward her and guided him into her. All his fantasies and dreams of sex were brushed away by the reality of being connected in this way to another person. He was eager to move in her but at the same time not completely sure how he should go about it.

"You remember where that shotgun is?" she said.

"Right beside us," he said.

"I'll listen out."

She began to move. He was relieved to let her set the rhythm. Then a mosquito buzzed in his ear. It was followed by another. He slapped at them.

"Can't fly this high?" he said.

She laughed.

"They're biting me too. Be quiet and concentrate."

The storm had moved off to the east, and the thunder gradually diminished. In the lightning flashes, he saw she had her head thrown back and her lips parted. The shotgun lay beside them. He wondered if she were actually listening for footsteps in the hallway.

Even as the mosquitoes swarmed about him, he was able to ignore their attacks. He came in a great rush. He looked down at her, and a lightning flash revealed she was smiling.

He rolled off her and lay on his back. They lay side by side for a long time until the sweat had dried on their bodies. Then they pulled the sheets over them against the attacks of the mosquitoes. The thunder was out of earshot now, the lightning reduced to a faint flicker on the horizon. She got up. He reached out and put his hand on her leg.

"Where are you going?" he asked.

"To look out the window," she said.

"Put some shoes on. Watch out for broken glass."

She did as he asked and went to the window. He heard the crunch of broken glass under her shoes.

"The stars are out," she said. "Come and look."

When he looked up at the sky, he saw it was clear. Then they heard laughter from the other end of the boat.

"I don't think they'll bother us," he said.

"Just keep that shotgun close."

They got back in the bed, neither of them bothering to put on clothes. He lay on his back, his hand on one of her breasts. It was too hot for any more contact than that. He waited to feel the sort of breathing from her that would mean she was asleep. But it never came.

"Can't you sleep?" he asked.

"Will you stand watch?" she asked.

He looked at his watch and saw there were three or four hours before sunrise.

"Sure," he said. "You go on to sleep."

"If they come, don't argue with them," she said. "Just kill them."

"Just like that?"

"Yes, before they do it to us."

He almost made a joke about that being an un-Christian thing to do but decided against it. He did not like having to contemplate harming Richard and Drexel. They had plucked them out of their sinking boat. Prison or their belief in God or some force, perhaps unknown even to them, had transformed them into good men. He did not care how many banks Drexel had robbed or that Richard's wife was dead by his hand. That was in the past.

Richard, if he were telling the truth, had probably not meant to kill his wife. Stephen recalled how Richard had observed it did not seem real that she was dead. He remembered his father and his killers lying on the sand, how that did not seem real.

Then he got up and put on his clothes. Taking the shotgun, he sat in a chair placed in a position that allowed him to have a view of both the window and the door. He supposed if they tried to force the door he would kill them. It would be a simple thing to do. Yet he hoped he would not have to do that.

Angela's breathing had fallen into the slow, heavy rhythm of sleep. To pass the time he began to count all the dead people he had seen floating in the water. Not a single one of them would receive a burial or even have the briefest word said over them. When he reached thirty, the count slowed down. But as he sat there, the images of the floating dead, some grotesque and some peaceful, kept forming in his mind. And he felt a vague sense of panic there would be no end to the count, that it would go on and on until he was exhausted. He would break his promise to Angela and sleep. The prisoners, whose characters he might have misread, would slip into the room, and he and Angela would join the floating dead.

TWELVE

Stephen opened his eyes. The room was full of light. He noticed the bed was level. It was clear to him that the water had risen, leveling the boat. Angela was still soundly sleeping. He wished they could take a bath together in the big Jacuzzi tub in the bathroom and then go down to the dining room for breakfast. In the evening they might go to the casino and gamble. Then they would return to the room and make love.

He slung the Saiga over his shoulder and moved the couch away from the door. He left Angela sleeping to go find the prisoners. He carefully opened door after door, but the rooms were all empty.

Out on deck he found them sleeping on mattresses they had dragged out there. They each had thrown a sheet over themselves to keep off the mosquitoes. He prodded Richard's leg with his foot. He knew it was Richard because his body made a larger mound under the sheet. Richard groaned and rolled over. An empty whiskey bottle was by his side. He wondered if they were still drunk.

"Get up," Stephen said.

Richard poked his head out from under the sheet. He rubbed his eyes and then took a look at the sun, which was just rising over a line of cypresses.

"Boy, it's mighty early to be getting a man up," he said.

"Water's rising," Stephen said. "You lay around in bed a little longer and we'll be floating down the river."

Now Drexel was stirring.

"Get up," Richard said. "You heard what this boy said."

Drexel emerged from beneath the sheet.

"I heard," he said. "How could I help not hear?"

"Can't hold his liquor," Richard said.

"Just as well as you," Drexel said.

He sat up and looked around.

"Where's the girl?" Drexel asked.

"Don't you be worrying about that girl," Richard said. "She's this boy's girl."

"No, that's not so," Stephen said.

But he hoped the opposite might be true. She had made love to him, but he realized she had probably done that with plenty of boys, every one of them a boy who believed in Jesus. They were not pretending as he had.

"I think she likes me," Drexel said.

Richard laughed.

"A college girl like that ain't gonna have nothing to do with you," he said.

"How do you know she's a college girl?" Drexel said.

"She told me," Richard said.

"Boy, is that true?" Drexel asked.

"That's what she says," Stephen said.

"Drexel, just put your mind off her," Richard said. "What we have got to do is find somebody to surrender to and show 'em we saved these children. Then maybe we'll see that pardon from the governor."

Stephen went back to wake Angela. Soon they were lowering themselves down the rope and into the bridge boat. Richard started the engines and took the helm. Drexel took a position in the bow to watch for snags. The pump jet kicked up a cloud of black mud.

"Look at that good black mud," Drexel said. "After the water goes down somebody's gonna grow them-selves a million dollars' worth of beans in this field."

"We don't get that pardon, we gonna be growing beans and cotton for free for the state of Louisiana for the rest of our natural lives," Richard said.

Richard steered the boat through the field as Drexel pointed out the places where there were snags.

They crossed a creek and then floated over the top of what Richard said was a private levee and into another enormous field with cypresses scattered here and there at one end. Richard began to wonder if it was mostly an oxbow lake instead of a field.

As the field or lake curved to the northeast, Richard followed the curve along the edge of the flooded timber. Then up ahead Stephen saw a boat anchored in their path. He looked through the field glasses and identified it as a towboat.

"Lost his barges," Richard said. "Maybe he's out of diesel."

Stephen scanned the deck of the towboat and saw there were figures on deck looking at them with field glasses.

"We'll have a look," Richard said. "Boy, you keep that shotgun close."

Stephen chambered a shell and took a position behind Richard. Drexel was looking at the towboat through the field glasses as they drew closer.

"Women!" he shouted. "Ain't nothing but women!"

Angela took the glasses from him and turned them on the towboat.

"He's right," she said.

Drexel snatched the glasses from her. They were now rapidly closing the distance between the two boats.

"Fine-looking women," Drexel said.

"You just remember we're looking for that pardon," Richard said. "You insult those women and we'll be back to chopping cotton."

"I'm not gonna insult nobody," Drexel said. "It's probably been a long time since they've seen a handsome man like me."

Now they were drawing close. Three women stood on the deck. One had a bullhorn in her hands.

"You prisoners stand off," a metallic voice came over the water.

"We standing off!" Richard shouted. He turned to Stephen and Angela. "Put down that shotgun and get up here where they can see you good."

Stephen and Angela climbed up beside Richard and Drexel.

"We rescued these children," Richard shouted. "We looking to give this boat back to the Corps."

"All right," the voice said. "Come alongside so we can have a look at you."

Stephen saw that one of the women had brought a machine gun out on deck. She was resting the barrel on the rail and covering them with the gun. Another woman was supporting the belt of cartridges.

Richard maneuvered the boat until it was alongside the towboat. The woman put down the bullhorn.

"I'm Captain Sullivan," she said. "This is the towboat *Sally James*. Keep your hands where Chandra can see them. I know you don't want to make her nervous. Now you come on aboard. Leave any weapons in your boat. Let the children come first."

"We ain't gonna do nothing to make Chandra nervous," Drexel said.

He gave her a big smile, but Chandra, a thin black woman, gave him no encouragement. She looked like she was ready to sweep the deck of the bridge boat with automatic fire at any moment.

Stephen and Angela boarded the boat.

"Are those prisoners telling the truth?" Captain Sullivan asked.

She was a black woman. She wore khaki pants and a shirt with her name stitched on it with red thread. On her belt was a big pistol in a holster.

"Yes, ma'am," Stephen said.

"They saved us," Angela said.

It turned out that the *Sally James* belonged to Captain Sullivan and her husband. They were both retired army officers. Her husband was somewhere between this point and New Orleans, looking for a string of runaway barges. He knew her position and would return as soon as he found them.

"Just because a few hurricanes show up don't mean it's the end of the world," she said. "Those barges are carrying soybeans worth a lot of money."

The women manning the machine gun were the deckhands Chandra and Mary Jane. It was all the crew she could put together on short notice. The towboat had what Captain Sullivan thought was a bent propeller shaft as a result of an encounter with a piece of debris in the river. She had managed to get the boat out of the river and over the submerged bank and levee and into the lake. When her husband Henry returned, he would tow them back upriver to Natchez.

"Hey, Captain," Drexel yelled. "Can we come aboard?"

Captain Sullivan looked them over one last time.

"What were you in Angola for?" she asked.

"Killed my wife," Richard said. "By mistake."

"Banks," Drexel said.

Then he grinned as if he were proud of that accomplishment.

Chandra and Mary Jane giggled.

"Get that boat tied up right," Captain Sullivan said. "Those convicts won't know how."

The deckhands put up the machine gun and caught the lines thrown to them by Drexel.

"We just want to surrender," said Richard.

"And get our pardon from the governor for saving these children," Drexel said.

"Come aboard," Captain Sullivan said. She tapped the butt of the pistol. "But I won't tolerate any foolishness."

"We believe you," Richard said.

They all climbed aboard.

Chandra made coffee. Then she stood off to one side with the machine gun. As they sat around a table, Captain Sullivan had Stephen and Angela tell the story of how they came to be on the bridge boat with the prisoners.

"Where'd you get that machine gun?" Richard asked.

"Belonged to the National Guard," Chandra said.

Mary Jane explained how they had come across a wrecked bridge boat with what looked like a hole made by a rocket launcher in the cockpit. The crew was dead.

"Strange nobody took this machine gun," Mary Jane said. "It was right there on the deck."

"Maybe they killed each other and the other boat just floated away," Richard said.

"We'll never know," Captain Sullivan said.

Stephen thought of the attack on the barge. He was wondering if Angela was thinking of that too. In that case too the dead had vanished.

"That's when I realized the rising river and tornadoes and hurricanes weren't what we should worry the most about," Captain Sullivan said. "It's people who're dangerous."

Captain Sullivan had talked with her husband on the radio the day before. He was going to look for the barges one more day and then return upriver. She had told him the bent propeller shaft had left her in a vulnerable position. The bridge boat with the dead soldiers had convinced her she should not stay in this isolated place too long. She wanted him to find those barges loaded with beans and hurry back.

There was power on the towboat and plenty of food in the galley. They all took showers and washed their clothes. Drexel and Richard were much too big to wear any of the women's clothes. But Stephen and Angela now wore some of Captain Sullivan's khakis. Both of them cut off the pants to make shorts.

Stephen noticed that Drexel was lavishing attention on Chandra and Mary Jane. Captain Sullivan had noticed it too, but she did not seem to mind.

"Look at that fool," Richard whispered to Stephen. "Thinks he's a ladies' man."

"You could show him how," Angela said.

"Those girls are too young for me," Richard said. "I've been in prison a long time. I'd need to go slow. Start with the right sort of woman."

Stephen wondered what that meant. When he had a chance, he asked Angela.

"Do you think he means prostitutes?" Stephen asked.

"I don't know," Angela said. "Maybe it's men he's used to."

Stephen wondered how it was for a man when, after all those years in prison, the opportunity to sleep with women presented itself.

They had a good evening meal. Chandra did the cooking. Drexel had three slices of her apple pie and praised every bite. Both Richard and Captain Sullivan were looking on him with amusement. After they ate, he helped her with the dishes.

Once it grew dark Stephen noticed Captain Sullivan allowed the lights on the boat to be turned on. He recalled how he and his father had elected to live in darkness. The illuminated boat would be visible for miles. Maybe she wanted it to be a beacon for her husband.

They sat around the table and talked until late. Captain Sullivan tried to contact her husband on the radio again but failed. She then raised a National Guard outpost and gave them their position. The radio operator said they could do nothing for them now but noted their position.

"That oxbow lake below Luke's Cuttoff," she said. "Are you writing that down?"

The radio operator told her he was.

Then Captain Sullivan set watches. The prisoners were not included in the rotation. She instructed them to go to a cabin and sleep.

"I catch you wandering about and I'll lock you in the engine room," she said.

Stephen was thankful that he would get to sleep unmolested by mosquitoes.

But when Mary Jane woke him for his watch, she told him that Drexel had stood Chandra's watch with her.

"Are you going to tell the Captain?" Stephen asked.

"No, I'd have to wake her up," she said. "Then she'd lock Drexel in the engine room. He don't mean no harm. Besides, Chandra likes him. Her brother's in prison. She ain't worried about him being a prisoner. He never hurt nobody."

Stephen walked about the deck with the Saiga. Now all the lights on the boat were off. He could see the sweep of the stars. Looking around him, he saw no lights in any direction. Somewhere out on the river Captain Sullivan's husband had found a place to moor the towboat. In the morning he would continue his search for the lost barges. And there were nervous National Guard soldiers standing watch along the perimeter of the flooded, lawless land.

Angela had told him to come to her bed and wake her after his watch. They were another couple on the boat who were going to devote the rest of the night to love.

THIRTEEN

They settled into a routine on the towboat. It was so pleasant to have good food. Chandra made ribs and chicken and dumplings, biscuits, cornbread, peach cobbler, fried okra and fried chicken. She was particularly good at fried chicken. Drexel said he could eat it for every meal.

"Down at Angola they wait until a chicken dies before they cook it," Drexel said.

And the watches were spread out enough so every night Stephen got plenty of mosquito-free sleep. After his watch he went straight to Angela's bed. He liked going to sleep with his hand resting between her legs or on a thigh or breast. He was still awkward at lovemaking, but Angela was patient. She claimed she didn't have that much experience herself. He wondered if she was telling the truth, but he thought it unwise to press her on the subject.

"So you think in four years I slept with every boy at LSU," he could imagine her saying.

It was obvious to everyone that Chandra and Drexel were lovers. Drexel praised her food, even if it was just a bowl of grits. He kept the kitchen clean for her.

As long as the water level stayed right where it was, they could wait on the towboat for a long time. They had plenty of water and fuel and food. The very best outcome would be for a military boat to appear on the lake and ferry them to safety. After watching the helicopter crash, he was not eager to be airlifted.

Captain Sullivan kept trying to reach her husband, but by the end of their fifth day on the boat she had heard nothing. She had no luck getting the National Guard or anyone else on the radio again.

"I wouldn't be surprised if he's gone all the way to Cuba to find those barges," she said.

They were sitting at the table for the evening meal, eating Chandra's fried catfish and slaw. She had used the last of the cabbage to make it.

"Yes, ma'am, I believe he would," Mary Jane said.

"Stephen, what's that ole Swamp Hog been saying these days?" Richard asked.

Richard told them about the prisoner who was broadcasting from some unknown location.

Stephen had not turned on the radio since they arrived at the towboat. It seemed to him that you needed to be out in the swamp to listen to the Swamp Hog, and he said this to the group.

"Yeah," Drexel said. "You need to be hungry and dirty and the mosquitoes all over you. That's when you dial him up. That crazy man will make you laugh and laugh."

On the boat's radio they heard the usual contradictory reports. Last night the governor had come on and asked everyone to remain calm, that soon order would be restored.

"Don't you give out all your pardons," Drexel said.

"That's the governor of Mississippi," Captain Sullivan pointed out.

Everyone laughed.

"Ask the Swamp Hog for a pardon," Richard said.

"You're looking for one too," Drexel said. "You children remember your story."

"I think the truth will do," Angela said.

"Drexel wants them to say that he wrestled an alligator as long as the bridge boat to save 'em," Richard said.

"There's some big gators out in them swamps," Drexel said.

"Dial in that station," Richard said.

Stephen stepped up to the radio that was on a shelf by the window.

He turned it on and tried, but there was only static.

"Use *your* radio," Angela said.

Stephen went to get the radio. When he returned, Angela was trying to find the station on the boat's radio but was having no success. Stephen cranked the generator and then spun the dial to the station. To his surprise the Swamp Hog's voice came in clearly.

"*Listen children,*" he said. "*The deluge ain't over. Great whales will swim through the French Market. Sharks are swimming through the streets of Lake Charles. I've seen 'em myself. Go inland. Don't stop until somebody offers you a ride on an elephant. In the western mountains. The jungle in Death Valley...*"

The voice abruptly descended into static.

"That's how it always is," Stephen said.

Captain Sullivan wondered where he was transmitting from.

"We've talked about that," Richard said. "It ain't the prison. That's underwater now."

"Duck Hill," Drexel said.

"Hush up," Richard said. "They don't want to listen to your crazy talk."

Chandra threw her arms about Drexel's neck.

"He ain't crazy," she said. "Tell us about Duck Hill."

"He's right," Drexel said. "I was just making up stories."

"You ain't been makin' up anything else to me?" she asked.

"No, ma'am," Drexel said. "No, ma'am."

"You better be telling me nothing but the truth," she said.

"That's all I can speak," Drexel said.

Richard laughed.

"He is truthful. Mostly."

Then Drexel got up to help Chandra with the dishes. Captain Sullivan set the watches and went off to bed. Mary Jane had the first watch. She took the machine gun, which had a short belt loaded into it, and went out on deck. Captain Sullivan had ordered enough lights to be left on so the boat would be easy for her husband to find in the dark. Angela went off to bed. Stephen lingered at the table with Richard.

"Pour me 'bout half a cup of coffee," Richard asked.

Stephen poured one for Richard and one for himself.

"Do you think the governor will give us that pardon?" Richard asked.

"I don't see why not," Stephen said. "After he hears what you did for us, he's certain to."

But Stephen realized he really knew nothing of the pardons. It seemed to him that Richard was a good man. He had had a lapse that cost his wife her life and him his freedom. He wondered how long ago that had been and what kind of man Richard was at that time.

Richard wrapped his big hands around the cup of coffee.

"I guess if I get that pardon, I'll go to Memphis and find me a woman," Richard said.

It turned out that was where he was born. His father worked for the railroad and made a good living.

"Memphis is probably full of refugees," Stephen said.

"I expect it is," Richard said.

Stephen wondered what the encounter between Richard and some prostitute would be like. It would be sad. Richard would be trying to make up for all those lost years with the hired body of some girl from a small town in Tennessee or Mississippi or Arkansas, a girl who had probably come to Memphis hoping for something else. He had once heard Josephine say something like that about prostitutes in New Orleans.

"Then what will you do?" Stephen asked.

"I know about farming," Richard said. "If I had some money, I'd buy me some land. But I won't be able to do that. I guess I'll work for somebody. Once the water goes down they'll need folks to help get the land back in shape. I can drive a tractor. Do a little work on engines."

Stephen thought of the paintings his mother was concerned about and how just one of them would buy

Richard a small farm. He imagined slipping back into New Orleans and making off with a painting.

Probably get shot by one of those mercenaries, he thought.

He looked through one of the windows and saw Mary Jane standing on the deck.

"Drexel's gonna have a hard time forgetting about Chandra if we don't get that pardon," Richard said.

Stephen imagined Chandra going to visit Drexel in some new prison. The water covering Angola might never recede.

"She won't be able to do nothing for him," Richard said. "She'll just have to get on with whatever she was doing before she met him."

"You'll be pardoned," Stephen said. "You've got to be."

"It's hard to accept things turning out different than you want. I put my hands on my wife. Drexel walked into a bank with a pistol. We weren't born at some other place or time, so we wouldn't have to do those things. We were at that place, at that time. Nobody else was there. Just us."

Stephen did not know what to say, so he said nothing. He wished Richard goodnight and went off to Angela's bed.

As he lay there with her in his arms, he found himself still thinking of Richard and Drexel.

"What's the matter?" she asked.

He told her about his conversation with Richard. And he added his fantasy of stealing one of his mother's paintings and selling it to buy Richard some land to farm.

"Shot by one of her mercenaries," she said.

"She'd probably shoot me herself if she caught me doing that," he said.

She laughed.

"I don't think so," she said. "But she'd be mighty mad. Military school would surely be waiting for you."

Then it was his turn to laugh.

"She finds out about me and I'll be chopping cotton with Richard and Drexel," she said. "You're underage."

"She'll be glad to be rid of me," he said.

"She loves you."

"I suppose."

"Now put all that out of your head and make love to me."

He wrapped his arms around her, determined to lose himself in the feel of her body against his. And he succeeded, both of them borne away to a place where the flood and the floating dead did not exist.

FOURTEEN

They continued to wait for the return of Captain Sullivan's husband. She had had no more contact with him on the radio. She kept making jokes that he had gone to Cuba in pursuit of the barges. But Stephen could tell she was worried. She complained about the food Chandra cooked. She questioned all of them about whether they were staying awake on their watches. She still did not allow the prisoners to stand watches.

"I could use more sleep," Chandra said.

"I'll decide who stands watch," Captain Sullivan said.

Stephen could tell that Chandra knew that was the end of the matter. He had heard Drexel telling Richard that as far as he was concerned they could stay on the towboat until Christmas. Richard had laughed and said he understood about that.

He lay in bed beside Angela, who was sound asleep. She mumbled something. He wrapped his arms around her and buried his face in the small of her back. She smelled of soap. Sweat too. It was an especially hot night. He decided to let her sleep. They could make love in the morning when it was cooler.

Suddenly he heard Captain Sullivan's voice yelling something. Then there was a shot, probably from her pistol, followed by automatic weapon fire. He guessed that was the machine gun. He picked up the Saiga, which he had slipped under the narrow bed. Angela was now awake.

"What's happening?" she asked.

"Don't know," he said. "Stay close."

After they slipped into their clothes, he eased the door open. There was more shooting and some shouts. He looked out the door and saw Mary Jane lying in a pool of blood in the hallway.

"Oh, Jesus," he said.

"What is it?" Angela asked.

"We're being attacked. They're on the boat. Get the dry bag."

At least he was prepared for this. He had packed ammo, the field glasses, water and some of the combat rations from the bridge boat in the dry bag.

He led her out of the cabin, and they went down the hallway, past the body of Mary Jane. Just then a man came running down the stairs from the deck. He carried an M-16 in his hands. Stephen brought up the Saiga and shot him in the chest. He did not ponder the death of the man.

They ran up the stairs past him. The deck was clear.

"Captain Sullivan," Angela said.

He saw her, obviously dead, lying by the rail, the machine gun beside her. They heard the sound of someone, more than one person, running on the deck. Stephen readied the shotgun, intending to shoot whoever it was when they came around the corner.

Then the people were before them, and Stephen swung the shotgun on them.

"Wait!" Richard shouted. "No!"

It was Richard, Chandra, and Drexel. They were unarmed.

"Get that machine gun," Stephen said.

They all glanced in the direction of Captain Sullivan's body. Drexel ran across the deck. As he stooped to pick up the machine gun, automatic weapon fire came from the water below. The rounds hit above their heads, making sharp pings against the metal structure of the boat. Drexel had flattened himself out against the deck.

"Stay put," Stephen said.

He crawled across the deck until he was beside Drexel. Then he looked over the edge and saw the outline of three johnboats. An outboard motor started and then another. Then there was a flash and a *whoosh*, followed by an explosion that made the whole boat shudder. Someone had fired a rocket launcher at the boat. There was another explosion, and a fire began to burn below them.

"Must've hit a fuel tank," Richard said. "Let's get off this boat."

Another round from the rocket launcher hit the pilot house. Stephen wondered if that was what the shooter was aiming at or if he had fired high. Then another motor started, and he heard the boat moving away from the towboat.

Drexel tugged at Stephen's shotgun.

"Kill those motherfuckers!" he screamed.

Stephen held onto the shotgun and pushed Drexel away.

"They're leaving," Stephen said. "Let 'em go."

Stephen did not want to press the people in the johnboats into a fight those left alive on the towboat might lose.

The bridge boat was on the other side of the towboat. They ran across the deck and found it still moored. As they slipped over the side, Chandra began to untie the lines. Richard started the engines.

They moved away from the towboat.

"Get us out of the light!" Stephen shouted. "Out of the light!"

Flames were shooting out of the superstructure of the towboat, as Richard took the boat out of the light and into the darkness.

Chandra was sobbing.

"They're all dead," she said. "All dead. Because of me."

"Hush up," Drexel was saying. "Hush up."

Now Richard was retracing the path they had taken to the towboat, running slowly by the edge of the timber in the darkness.

Angela had gone over to sit next to Chandra. Drexel was beside Richard in the cockpit. Angela talked with Chandra a long time, then hugged her and returned to Stephen. Chandra went to stand beside Drexel, who put his arm around her.

"She wasn't standing her watch," she said. "Drexel came up on deck and they went down to her cabin. That's how those people took us by surprise."

But someone, either Captain Sullivan or Mary Jane, was awake or had been awakened. Captain Sullivan was preparing to use the machine gun when someone killed her. Perhaps Mary Jane was on her way to the deck to feed the gun for Captain Sullivan.

They crossed the sunken levee and descended into a swamp where it was hard to maneuver the bridge boat in the darkness. They all agreed it was not prudent to show lights. Finally they found a open space and moored the boat.

Once the watches were set, they lay down to sleep. The mosquitoes were especially bad, and they were running out of repellent.

"I was gonna fix fried chicken today," Chandra said. "And now these mosquitoes are eating me up."

"I'm trying not to think about any fried chicken," Richard said as he slapped at a mosquito.

Drexel turned to Stephen.

"I saw you put the hurt on that man in the hall. You're a mean man with that shotgun."

Stephen recalled for the first time that the man had a bulge in his cheek. Tobacco, gum, an infection. He would never know. He hoped that image would quickly fade and be lost, and in his dreams there would only be an indistinct, featureless figure in the hall: a big white man dressed in cutoff blue jeans.

"You're the man," Drexel continued.

"Let it be," Angela said.

"He's too young to be killing folks," Chandra said.

"But not for loving," Richard said.

They all laughed.

Stephen pretended to be embarrassed, but actually he was glad that the conversation had turned away from the dead man.

As Stephen stood in the cockpit on the first watch, he thought of Chandra's fried chicken. They had almost nothing in the way of provisions now. They were especially low on water, the big water cooler only half full. Five people would go through that in a hurry on a hot day. He had two full canteens in the dry bag. No one had thought to prepare the bridge boat for an escape.

They were going to have to find some high ground, a National Guard outpost, someplace where they would be safe.

In the morning Stephen woke to see Chandra standing her watch.

"I'm right here," she said. "I'm awake."

Then the others woke.

They decided to move to the northeast. When they came out of the swamp, Richard steered the boat through the field as Drexel pointed out snags. At the edge of the field, they found passage into a creek. Richard steered the boat into an eddy, and they all discussed the best way to proceed.

"I thought we'd decided to go northeast," Stephen said.

Drexel was for going down the creek to the river. Richard argued against that. He believed they were too low on fuel to risk dealing with the river.

"We'll need to go upstream," Richard said. "But this diesel won't last long if we have to run the engines hard.

Look what happened to that towboat. Probably two towboats. I don't expect that Mr. Sullivan is ever coming back."

The creek did not present that sort of problem since there was little current in it. Stephen and Angela and Chandra agreed with Richard.

"We get lucky and this creek'll take us to high ground," Richard said.

They started up the creek, at this point close to the river at least a hundred yards wide. And it held that length as they slowly made their way through a labyrinth of snags and an occasional fallen tree.

It was close to dark when they saw a pine-covered ridge. A bat twisted overhead. The creek narrowed. Then far across an immense flooded field Stephen saw a collection of army trucks parked on an asphalt road where it disappeared into the flooded field. Soldiers were standing around. Coils of barbed wire were strung between the water and the road. When he looked at the road through the field glasses, he counted perhaps a dozen soldiers. They had heard the sound of the boat's engines and were looking toward them. They were all in uniform. A certain order to their position made him believe this was the army and not some collection of deserters.

Drexel stood up on the bow and waved his hands and whooped. Stephen doubted that they could hear him over the sound of the engines. From the cockpit Richard was also waving at the soldiers. He turned the boat out of the creek and into the flooded field.

"We're gonna get that pardon," Drexel shouted.

"I believe you will," Chandra said.

Stephen wondered just exactly what Chandra had pictured for the future. Marriage to Drexel? Children? He wondered if Drexel would go back to robbing banks.

"You children remember to tell them soldiers how we took care of you," Richard said.

They were halfway across the field.

"You watching the water?" Richard yelled to Drexel.

"I'm watching," Drexel said.

Stephen swept his glasses over the army position. The soldiers who had been standing about behind the wire had disappeared.

Then Drexel, who was standing up and waving, suddenly sailed backward and landed on the metal deck. A moment later they all heard the sound of the shot, an elongated sound held in by the high ground on three sides. Richard turned his head to see what had happened to Drexel. As he did he pitched backward to join him, the sound of the rifle shot arriving a moment later.

"Oh, God!" Angela was screaming. "Oh, God!"

"Lord! Lord!" Chandra screamed.

She threw herself on Drexel and pulled him close to her as if she were trying to will life back into him.

The boat veered off to the left and Stephen, keeping his head below the edge of the cockpit, grabbed the wheel and turned the boat back toward the creek. Now all the soldiers were shooting at them. The rounds pinged against the metal hull. A few red tracers sailed by, glowing in the darkness.

Stephen took the boat back to the creek. By this time they were out of sight of the army position and no longer presented a target. He brought the boat into an eddy next to the bank and cut back the engines.

"Why did they do that?" Angela asked.

"They're scared," Stephen said. "They saw those prison uniforms and were afraid to take chances."

Chandra was still lying on top of Drexel.

"Go talk to her," he said.

She went over to Chandra and bent over her. She appeared to be whispering something to her.

"Is she all right?" he asked.

She turned and looked toward him, her face indistinct in the darkness.

"She's dead," she said.

Chandra had caught a bullet in the head as they were retreating across the field to the creek.

Together they slid the bodies of the prisoners and Chandra into the water.

How can this be? he thought. *They were alive one moment and dead the next. Their desire for pardons and love now a cruel joke.*

Angela prayed to Jesus to be on the lookout for the souls of the prisoners, that they were good men who had been punished enough on earth for their crimes. Stephen said "Amen" with her at the end of the prayer.

"She sure could cook fried chicken," Stephen said.

"She could," Angela said.

"Richard and Drexel were good men," he said.

"I'd never have thought I'd think that about a murderer and a bank robber," Angela said.

It was dark now. For a moment or two they could see the solid shape of the bodies, but these soon blended with the general darkness of the creek and were gone.

He hoped they would not come upon them in the morning, caught up on some snag. He wished them free and unimpeded passage to the Gulf, untouched by catfish or turtles. Their bones would lie on fine white sand, undisturbed in the clear, sunlit coastal waters. He imagined shafts of golden sunlight falling on them. Like something out of a dream.

"Like a cathedral," he said.

"What?" she asked.

So he told her of his vision.

"I like that," she said. "That's nice. I think Jesus will forgive them."

"He should," he said.

He wished that could be the fate of all the floating dead. Forgiven. Their bones lying in perfect symmetry in the clear water.

"What should we do?" Angela asked.

"We'll go back to the river," Stephen said.

"I thought we didn't have enough fuel."

"Not for going upstream. But we can go down. I think we have a good chance of getting to Mr. Parker's. Then we we can come back up this way with him and Holly in his johnboat."

So they moored the boat to the riverbank trees and went to sleep, dividing the night into the usual watches. Even if they sent up a helicopter in the morning, it was going to be hard to see the boat under the tree cover.

Stephen took the first watch and sat in the cockpit with the Saiga. Angela curled up on the metal deck.

As he scanned the upstream darkness, he thought of the burial of the prisoners and Chandra. Angela had cried and prayed. But he had felt nothing. His only regret was that they could not provide them a proper burial. No trip to the Gulf for them. His hopes for that were just a dream. Now they were part of the floating dead, destined to be eaten by catfish and turtles. What they didn't eat would sink to the bottom of the creek to become part of that rich black mud.

He felt what he thought was love for Angela. And perhaps if he concentrated hard enough on that, he would be saved. Not love for Jesus. He believed in none of that, despite Angela's words and her hopes for the souls of the dead.

"Saved for what," he said out loud.

His words sounded empty in the darkness, and he was afraid.

FIFTEEN

The river stretched a mile wide, maybe more, to a tree-covered shoreline. Beyond the half-submerged trees, perhaps half a mile away, was the levee, which he imagined was broken in many places on both the east and west banks. Where the creek entered the much stronger current of the river, there were some standing waves that might have swamped a johnboat, but for the bridge boat they were no problem.

His plan was to select a levee break on the east side of the river and hope it would lead them into the big field that held the Indian mound. All they could do was guess, but at least they were heading in the right direction. They would just have to be careful not to go too far downriver.

They clung close to the east bank to avoid the strong midriver currents. They saw no boats, only debris: houses, furniture, farm buildings, dead animals. He decided not to take the first break they came upon, while Angela was for taking it.

"We're going to end up in the Gulf," she said.

"Just remember how long it took to get through those swamps and flooded fields," he said. "We've got to conserve fuel."

But he realized she was right about overshooting. So he turned the boat into the next levee break. It was a wild ride through the flooded timber and then the break itself, with a big standing wave that would also have swamped the johnboat. Now they were down to a single barrel of diesel and whatever was left in the boat's fuel tank.

They spent the day working their way through a swamp and then into a big field that turned out not to be the right one. They spent the night in the field. The next day they had a hard time making their way through another swamp because of underbrush blocking the way to the south.

But late that afternoon they finally made it out of the swamp and into a field. They came around a timber-covered point, and there ahead was the mound and the house and trees rising out of the water.

When they drew closer, they saw the skiff. The kayak and the second johnboat were gone.

They moored the bridge boat and started up the hill to the house.

"I wonder where they went?" Angela asked.

"I have no idea," Stephen said.

"Why would they take the johnboat *and* the kayak?"

"Don't know that either."

Stephen checked the Saiga to make sure there was a round in the chamber.

"Look, there's no other boat here," he said. "It's just Mr. Parker and Holly."

"Yes, that's because someone has come and gone," Angela said.

As he approached the house and nobody came out to meet them, he unslung the Saiga. He told Angela to stay outside.

"What difference does it make," she said. "We both know what we're going to find in there."

He hoped he would find them sitting at the table on the screened porch. But when they approached the open door, he smelled death.

Mr. Parker lay just inside the door, a rifle beside him. This time Angela did not cry or scream. She did put the bottom of her T-shirt over her mouth and nose. They found Holly's naked body on the porch. Someone had slit her throat.

"They're better in the water," Angela said. "Don't stink so much."

Stephen told himself he should not be surprised at her detached reaction. They had both simply grown used to loss and the dead. Perhaps his father would be proved right. Death would replace love. For the first time he realized his father had been speaking of himself. He pitied him. He pitied himself and Angela. Only the dead were free.

Angela left him and walked back into the house.

"Where are you going?" he asked.

"To cover him up," she said.

Whoever had done it had taken food from the freezer and drained all the gas out of the generator tank. There was water in the cistern Mr. Parker had improvised out of sheet metal. Empty plastic jerry cans Mr. Parker had stockpiled were scattered about on the floor. The killers had taken all they could carry. Stephen expected the gasoline from the tank by the garage was all gone, but that would do them no good anyway. They needed diesel. The big farm shop and the diesel tank beside it were underwater.

When Angela returned, her face was pale and she walked unsteadily.

"You all right?" he asked.

"Give me a little while," she said. "I'll be fine."

"We'll take the skiff."

"It's tiny. And it leaks."

He told her he thought he could repair it.

"We'll need another paddle," he said. "Maybe some oars. I can make some in Mr. Parker's little shop."

"We'll spend the night here?" she asked.

"We have to. It'll be dark by the time I finish."

"We could go in the dark."

"Not a good idea."

He did not blame her. He did not look forward to spending the night among the dead.

They set to work on the skiff. He rigged some oarlocks. The skiff had been designed to be sculled through the narrow twisting pathways of cypress swamps, but he thought that a set of oars would be useful and more efficient on the rivers and creeks and when they had to cross immense flooded fields. He made the oars using a drawknife and some cypress planks he took off the wall of Mr. Parker's shop.

The rest of the afternoon they spent caulking the skiff. They would scull, row and perhaps pole it through the swamps and flooded creeks to high ground. They decided that they would put the skiff on the bridge boat or tow it behind. By using the diesel they had left, they would get as close to high ground as possible. They would approach any checkpoint in the skiff, not the bridge boat. This time the soldiers would take one look at them and know they were refugees, not criminals.

"It'll still leak a little," he said. "But not like before."

"These mosquitoes are going to eat us up tonight," she said.

"As near as I can tell they've been doing that most every night."

She glanced up the hill in the direction of the house.

"I don't think that porch is a good place to sleep," he said.

"We could bury her," she said.

"I guess we'll have to decide which is harder."

They sat on the skiff and discussed the best way to deal with Holly's body. The smell was not so bad on the porch. They could close the doors to the interior of the house and use the porch door.

"You ever done any grave digging?" he asked.

"You know I haven't," she said.

"It's going to be hard work."

"We don't have to exactly bury her," she said.

Her plan was to wrap the body in a plastic tarp and drag it well away from the house.

That seemed like a good idea to him. Who knew how many nights they would have to spend in the skiff? It would be pleasant to have one last mosquito-free night.

"Those mosquitoes have just about sucked every drop of blood out of my body," he said.

"Let's do it," she said.

It turned out not to be as hard as he expected. It was fairly easy for the two of them to tow the slick plastic across the grass. They left her under a fig tree next to the garage. The sink of death mixed with the scent of the ripe figs. Wasps and yellow jackets were doing a good business with the fruit that had fallen to the ground and begun to rot.

They quickly filled a plastic bin with fresh figs from the tree.

Before they left, Angela insisted on saying some words over Holly. He felt foolish standing there with his cap full of figs while she prayed to Jesus. When she said "Amen" he said it too, and he could tell she was pleased with that.

"She'll rest softly right here under this tree," she said.

"Yes, I believe she will," he said.

They returned to the porch. The smell was still strong, but as it grew dark a little breeze came up from the river and made it somewhat better.

"I wish we had some incense," Angela said.

"You'd need a pile of incense," he said.

By the time they had supper, they had either got used to the stink or the breeze had carried it away (he could not tell which). Once it grew dark he was glad he had listened to Angela. He looked forward to a sleep uninterrupted by mosquitoes.

"We should stand watches," he said.

"If we don't, I won't be able to sleep," she said.

If someone came by in the night, they would come looking for the keys to the bridge boat.

"I wonder if Mr. Parker's wife is in Baton Rouge," he said.

"I hope she's been evacuated," she said.

He considered what it was going to be like for her to come back to the house after the water had gone down and order was restored and the dead were buried. The smell of death would be long gone. The rattlesnakes and copperheads would have returned to the woods.

"Or dead," he said.

"No, I like to think of her in Memphis," she said. "That's good high ground."

She looked out into the darkness beyond the screen.

"Do you think we covered her up enough?" she asked.

"We wrapped that tarp pretty tight," he said.

He considered what might get at her: possums, feral cats, a coyote. But he had seen none of those animals on the mound. He recalled how Hector's body was preserved from decay in *The Iliad*. He wondered if Jesus had ever done something like that. He had never read any of *The New Testament*. He was reluctant to ask Angela. He did not want to get her started on Jesus.

"Vultures won't be able to bother her?" she asked.

"I don't think so," he said.

It seemed to him that he should be able to say something about the dead that would make them, the living, feel better. But there was nothing to say. There was no possibility of revenge and certainly no possibility of their unknown killers being brought to justice. There was a possibility that in the violent world of the flooded land, the killers themselves had already met a similar fate. He had extracted a certain measure of justice on his father's killers. He wondered how he would now handle the redheaded man's surrender.

"I let one of my father's killers escape," he said.

She asked him to explain.

"I would've done the same thing," she said.

"Now?"

"I don't know about now."

She paused for a moment.

"But maybe I would," she said. "Maybe I would. And you?"

"I think that now I would've pulled the trigger," he said.

"And felt bad about it later."

"No, I'd feel nothing at all."

"Nothing?"

"Yes, I think that's what I'd feel."

He recalled his father's warning. But he was certain that he could love. He loved Angela.

He hoped she would not start talking about Jesus, and she did not. She simply sighed. Then she asked him to get out the radio.

They pulled in a few stations and heard about a riot in a refugee camp in Natchez and the usual contradictory reports about the water going up or down. No one mentioned anything about the situation in Baton Rouge, just that the flooded parts of the country were in a state of anarchy and chaos.

"I can't imagine Americans doing what they've been doing," the announcer from a Texas station said.

"Find the mystery station," Angela said.

He turned the dial. Several tries gained him only a few scattered words from the Swamp Hog. But then the station came in clearly.

"*The Rocky Mountains are gonna be a jungle*," the voice said. "*Two hundred inches of rain a year. Palm trees, banyan trees, elephant grass. Big, big trees festooned with vines. Parrots, monkeys, tigers, peacocks, elephants, cobras.*"

The list of animals and birds went on and on, finally trailing off into static.

"He's crazy," Stephen said.

"Maybe there's some truth to it," she said.

"All those animals?"

"No, the Rocky Mountains becoming covered with jungle."

He made several more tries to find the station but had no luck. She went to sleep. He spent his watch with the radio, listening to tales of confusion and despair.

SIXTEEN

They made a skidway of saplings and used a block and tackle he found in the garage to pull the skiff up onto the bridge boat. Then he told Angela the plan he had made during his last watch. They would cross the river in the bridge boat, go through a levee break on the west bank, and run the bridge boat on a westward course as far as the fuel lasted or until they were in the vicinity of high ground. Then they would abandon it for the skiff.

"Why the other side of the river?" she asked.

"I want to go to the Rockies," he said.

"You've been paying too much attention to the Swamp Hog."

"There're no hurricanes in the Rocky Mountains."

"It doesn't matter to me. I just want to get to high ground. And what about going to Baton Rouge to find your mother?"

"There's not enough fuel to do it in the bridge boat. We'll never make it in the skiff."

"You can find her later."

"I will."

He was pleased she had shown good sense about their options.

They ran the boat across the field and then through a swamp and through a levee break. This one had a strong current, but the bridge boat had no problem overcoming it.

After they crossed the river, they hugged the slack water next to the bank for several miles, looking for a break in the levee or a place where it had been over-topped. They ended up in a flooded field. It was easy to set a course due west into the afternoon sun. By evening they were making their way through a swamp and running low on diesel. They moored the boat to a tree and spent the night.

In the morning they abandoned the bridge boat for the skiff. It was going to be much easier maneuvering the skiff through the swamp, and he calculated that they had only a few minutes of fuel left anyway. After the time they had spent on the bridge boat, the skiff seemed impossibly small and fragile. It would never survive passage through a levee break. In the swamps he sculled it through the labyrinth of cypresses. In the flooded fields they took turns with the oars.

"How far do you think we'll have to go?" she asked.

"Ten miles, fifteen miles before we hit high ground," he said.

"But you're just guessing?"

"I'm guessing."

Since they had crossed the river, they had not seen a dead body. They had come upon a few dead animals, both wild and domestic. There had been one place where it looked like the entire population of a chicken house had drowned, the brown water covered with a mass of white-feathered swollen carcasses. The smell was bad.

They spent a night in the skiff and in the morning pressed on. They were running low on water. The weather was extremely hot and humid, but at least it was not raining. The flat, still expanse of brown water lay under a perfectly blue sky. They heard no noises that indicated other humans were about, no motors or gunshots or voices. No planes flew over.

In the middle of the afternoon, after they emerged from a swamp, he saw a pine-covered ridge ahead. Their hands were now blistered from rowing.

He scanned the ridge with the field glasses but saw no sign of anyone.

"No one will bother us," he said. "We don't look dangerous."

Then he saw a highway sign. It had the name of a town on it and the mileage. Only a few feet of water was over the road, and they followed it toward the ridge that now rose above them to the west.

Late in the afternoon the road began to emerge from the water as the land rose. They came upon a car that rested across the road, upside down. There were no bodies in it, no possessions. The interior was filled with mud.

Now there was barely enough water to float the skiff. It kept grounding out on the asphalt. So they got out of the boat and towed it. It was difficult walking because the road beneath their feet was slick with mud.

Then the road emerged from the water. They could see where it ascended the side of the ridge perhaps a quarter of a mile away. They left the skiff behind. Angela carried the dry bag with what little water and food they had left. He slung the Saiga over his shoulder. At any moment he expected one or both of them to fall, the victim of some hidden rifleman.

But when they reached the place on the road where the flood had not risen, it became clear that there had never been an army outpost here. In fact, it looked like no one had ever stopped a car or truck at this point on the highway.

They walked to the top of the hill. Off to the west was ridge after ridge of pines. Behind them the flooded land stretched off toward the river. The wind soughed in the pines as they stood in a spot of shade, the acrid scent of the trees spilling over them, a welcome change from the stink of mud. Even in the shade it was hot.

"Are you really thinking about going to the Rockies?" she asked.

"You heard the Swamp Hog," he said. "There're elephants in those mountains now."

She laughed. "You're talking crazy like him," she said.

"You'll see," he said. "There'll be elephants in those mountains one day."

And perhaps love too. Perhaps she would stay with him there, ignore the difference in their ages. He imagined riding an elephant with her through the streets of a little town, the animal's ponderous body swaying beneath them, the buildings strung with colored lights and everywhere soft music—guitars and flutes.

"I'll locate my mother," he said. "Let her know where we are."

"You can't locate her," she said.

"I know it's going to be hard."

"It's not that. She's dead."

He stopped and looked at her. This was not something she would joke about.

"You can't know that," he said. "Did Jesus tell you?"

She began to cry, and he immediately regretted he had spoken so harshly. He put his arms around her and told her he was sorry. She calmed down and wiped her face with her T-shirt.

"I saw her," she said. "When I went to look in the other rooms in Mr. Parker's house. She was lying there with a dead man. He was dressed in camouflage. I guess he was one of her security guards. I recognized her from that picture I saw at your father's house."

He sat down on the side of the road and she beside him.

"Why didn't you tell me?" he said.

"You had too much on your mind," she said. "Too many things you had to do right so we could stay alive."

"I could've buried her."

"Somebody will."

"Maybe."

"Did you say any words over her?"

He was immediately sorry he had asked her the question. He hoped she would not start talking about Jesus.

"No."

He considered what it would take to make the journey back to the house. It was not a journey he was seriously thinking of making. At least she would not become one of the nameless floating dead. She would be spared that. For some reason he thought of the wasps busy among the rotting fruit.

He sat there with her beside him, her arm about him, and wept softly. He had the sensation of vertigo as if he had slipped over a precipice and was falling to his death. He laid his head in her lap, and she stroked his hair.

"I wonder what she was doing there," he said.

"Maybe looking for you," she said.

He liked the idea of his mother looking for him. He wondered if his father would have believed that was her motive for being there.

"Anna just can't pay attention to anyone but herself," his father had once said.

That was when she was talking about sending him away to school. But she could have changed, especially after having been separated from him for the summer, perhaps acting on some scrap of information her mercenaries had discovered about his location. He wondered why he did not hold his father's absence against him. After all, his mother had raised him. What was worse: her indifference or his absence? It was hard for him to decide.

"What are you thinking?" she asked.

"About my parents."

She paused as if she was having a hard time considering what to say.

"No telling what's up ahead," she said.

"We can't go the other way," he said.

He sat up and wiped his eyes. He imagined them walking along the road. He did not expect them to come out of that walk alive. To walk over the crest of a hill and see the red-haired man standing there would come almost as a relief. If that happened, he would not hesitate this time, would show no mercy. That they were free of the violent life they had experienced on the flooded land was not something he was ready to accept. But he said nothing of this to Angela.

Despite the death of his mother and father, despite the deaths of Mr. Parker and Holly and Fred, the prisoners, the towboat crew and all the unknown floating dead, he felt a sense of excitement. They were on high ground. The mountains lay to the west.

They took up their gear and started down the road. He slung the Saiga. As they crested ridge top after ridge top, they saw only more pines.

"I'm not stopping until I see an elephant," Angela said.

Then she ran ahead of him, laughing, while he, the heavy shotgun banging against his back, ran after her.

SCOTT ELY received his MFA from the University of Arkansas and now teaches writing at Winthrop University in South Carolina. He has published five novels and four collections of short stories. *The Elephant Mountains* is his first novel for young adult readers. He lives in Rock Hill, South Carolina, with his wife, poet Susan Ludvigson, and several dogs.